PIERS DIAMOND

a novel by

MONICA SHALLIS

Published in 2016 by:

Cygnet New Scripts
Cygnet Theatre
Friars Gate
Exeter
EX2 4AZ

01392 425777
eaglearts@btinternet.com

ISBN: 978-1-539367-35-2

Typeset in Minion Pro

For Abigail

Foreword

The legacy of Monica Shallis is not complete without taking into account her enormous written and musical output, most of which remains unpublished. She founded Cygnet Training Theatre in the early 1980s and was its Artistic Director until her death in 2006. *Piers Diamond*, written during her final illness, has uncanny relevance today. Its futuristic setting – England now and yet not now, almost familiar but equally alien – and its 'cloak and dagger' plot, involving many themes of our time, with some remarkable twists and a subtle humour, make it eminently readable. In short, 'a jolly good yarn'!

We hope you enjoy this adventure.

Mary G Evans
for Cygnet New Scripts

1~

'Is Esmeralda on board?'

'Of course, First Minister.' As he replied the security man's lips curled in a fleeting smile of amusement and conspiracy. He resumed his seat beside the First Minister unable to prevent his face from showing just the merest hint of pleasure at being on the inside of a secret shared with the most important man in the world.

'Be careful,' Piers Diamond said quietly.

'I am - always.'

'Your face will give you away one day. Take care not to enjoy our little joke too openly, David.'

'I've never dropped you in it yet. I'm not going to start now. I'm employed to protect you, for Christ's sake. I'm not likely to forget that.'

'Me and Esmeralda.'

'You and Esmeralda.' Both men laughed and the First Minister returned his attention to the sheaf of papers in front of him.

On the short flight from Geneva to London the ministerial plane had hit some turbulence. Despite his exalted position as leader of the world parliament, Piers Diamond hated flying. As a child he had always been travel-sick. In adult life, and especially now, he took precautions but this did not stop his dread of journeys. The people who greeted him, or gathered to see him arrive at airports all over the world, had no idea what the flight had sometimes cost him. The small, hydrogen-powered plane in which he travelled lacked nothing in terms of comfort except stability. Piers sometimes wondered if the huge unwieldy jumbo jets of the past had been more comfortable. He could, if he wished to do so, instigate the reintroduction of a petrol-fuelled plane as an occasional, one-off extravagance for his own use. If history was to be believed the whole World Parliament could have been transported in one of them. But the waste represented by the unnecessary use of fossil fuels and the resultant damage to the environment made such a consideration impossible. It was up to him to set the best possible example, not to flout the gas emission limits for his own convenience. And then there were the safety considerations. Members of the World Parliament were even more careful than members of national governments to avoid travelling together. This was an essential security measure against the devastation of accident or engine failure.

The plane was flying smoothly now. The steward came towards them walking steadily on the thick-pile carpet. He leant down deferentially offering, as always, coffee, spirits, champagne. Piers, as always, declined all three. He tried to focus on the nuclear waste issues discussed in the set of papers in front of him. Reading on a plane tended to increase the danger of nausea. It was a problem. David Mason at his side, stretched and yawned. He was very much at ease with the First Minister. More so than most people dared to be. Piers Diamond was a brilliant man. He was a natural introvert with an enigmatically withdrawn nature and yet, paradoxically, he was a superb public speaker. This was partly due to the fact that he never saw any reason, in public or in private, to be other than sincere and direct. He was adored and trusted throughout the world for his confident handling of world affairs and for his good looks. Women dreamed of winning his love, men often angled for his friendship but Piers remained aloof. He had one failed marriage behind him and he never spoke of that. Nowadays he preferred to be alone.

David Mason was closer to Piers than almost anyone and yet he would have hesitated to claim that he had Piers' friendship. Sitting side by side on the plane they looked an ill-assorted pair. David was big and fleshy with a heavy jaw and a strong, thick neck and close cropped hair. He was armed of course, as were the other body-guards in his team who sat, stood or walked behind the First Minister at all times. David usually walked at his side.

Piers Diamond himself was fine boned and delicate. He was not tall, though people seeing him on television or even in the flesh gained the impression that he was well above average height. His hair was very dark, so were his eyes. His skin had a pale olive tint inherited from his Indian mother. He had also inherited her bone structure. She had been a great beauty. His English father had been an illustrious diplomat and had married his Indian bride during a period as British Ambassador to India. Piers had been born in India but was sent to school in England and when his mother died and his broken hearted father returned home he was only nine years old.

Aware that Piers was not reading but staring into space David chanced the moment to ask something that had been hovering in his mind ever since he began working for the First Minister.

'Do you enjoy going back to England?'

'Yes,' said Piers, 'Yes, I do.'

'Do you consider yourself English rather than Indian?'

'Oh, yes. I was at school in England from the age of six and my father moved back there when I was nine. That's where my roots are.'

'Do you still have family there?'

'Yes, in a way. My father's dead now but I have a step brother and sister still living.'

'Still living? That's a funny choice of words. Are you expecting them to pop off too?'

'Not exactly but Eden, my half-brother, lives as a bit of an Outsider and he drags Prunella my half-sister with him. I never know where they are from one year's end to the next. It's not a very satisfactory state of things, but I can't tell him how to live his life.'

'What about her?'

'It's not really up to her. She was born with Down's Syndrome, poor kid. Eden has taken responsibility for her after a fashion but the trouble is, he's a sort of adventurer who lives by his wits. I sometimes wonder if he's capable of being responsible for himself.'

'Some kind of maverick, is he?'

'You could say that. If it wasn't for Una, Prune's godmother, who steps in and looks after her when Eden goes off on one of his jaunts, I don't know what would happen.'

'No wonder you never say a word about your relations.'

'I'm not ashamed of them. It's simply that I hardly have a chance to see them these days. So there's a gulf. . . '

'I'll say there is!'

'But I do worry about little Prune.'

'Prune?'

'Prunella. That's her name, my funny little sister.'

'You don't see Down's Syndrome children these days. I thought it had been completely wiped out.'

'By abortion, you mean.'

'I don't know. I guess that's how they prevent it?'

'Yes. But my stepmother refused to agree to it. She was a law unto herself. She refused absolutely to have the pregnancy terminated when Prune was on the way. Which was sad, because, as well as having a Down's Syndrome baby, she contracted the Cranes-Patterson virus and died very soon after giving birth to Prune.'

'That's such a terrible thing. Haven't they found a cure for it?'

'Not yet. We've put a lot of money into the research but so far nothing has cracked it. It's one of the plagues of the third millennium.'

'Were you close to your step-mother?'

'No.'

'Was she all right, as a step-mother, I mean?'

'I hardly knew her. I was ten when my father remarried. I hated the idea but I was at boarding school and then at Oxford. By the time my education was finished she was dead and I had a half-brother and sister I hardly knew. They didn't interest me much, I'm sorry to say. I was obsessed with philosophy and politics, world issues, the sort of things I live and breathe today. I was twelve when Eden was born. He was a blond-haired angel of a child. My father indulged him. I was like a stranger in the house. School was my home. I found like minds there, people I could respect and love. I didn't want to go home after my father remarried and I wanted it even less with Eden on the scene.'

'And Prunella?'

'Oh, she was a very late arrival. As I said my step-mother was adamant about having her and loving her just as she was. But both she and my father were really rather old for having children by then.'

'Hence the Down's Syndrome.'

'It may be so, yes. Science has since confirmed the dangers of women bearing children late in life. My father was not young when he married my mother. He was really getting on when he married for the second time. And Myra, his second wife was not young herself. It was rather a misfortune that she became pregnant with Prune.'

'Not a happy event.'

'No, as it turned out, rather a tragic one.' Piers returned to his papers. There was silence for a while. Eventually David said,

'Will you see them?'

'Who?'

'Eden and Prunella - while you're in England.'

'It's very unlikely. I have no plans to do so.'

'They're not the reason for Esmeralda, then.'

'Good heavens, no!'

The previously silent plane suddenly began to vibrate with the metallic sound of the copter blades opening out above them. The noise level in a vertical landing was such that passengers were provided with ear protectors. Piers and David now reached for these and, of necessity, conversation ceased.

At the bottom of the small flight of steps from the plane the reception party and the press, held back behind their barriers, waited in the breezy summer sunshine. Piers smoothed his hair and straightened his jacket. David and his team checked their guns. The little party descended from the plane into the accustomed glare of public scrutiny.

2~

Eden was not a wealthy man. He lived with Prune in a small, rather derelict house in the Outsider district known as Wimbledon Common. The house stood by itself among trees and had a secure iron fence. Eden liked a bit of space around him. It was a shabby house both inside and out. Eden was not a home-maker, he was a collector, an adventurer, a go-getter. He lived on his wits and enjoyed the challenge of generating an income for the sole purpose of being free to do what he chose to do. He was not above fleecing rich Insiders if he got the chance. He considered them fair game. He drew the line at fleecing Prune, who had an allowance from Piers that was both generous and reliable, but he was not unwilling to let her income cover their living expenses. He felt this to be fair, since he was shouldering the burden of looking after her while Piers disported himself on the world stage, coining in millions from his best selling books on Politics and Philosophy. Prune's contribution to their lifestyle was, after all, nothing more than a reasonable rent.

Prune never thought to question whether the rent she paid for living in Outsider squalor with Eden was reasonable. Eden had obtained all the necessary bank documents and a tidy sum was transferred from Prune's healthy account to his unhealthy one in the first week of every month. Prune was very happy, Eden was fairly happy and Piers knew nothing about it.

They knocked along without too much trouble. Neither of them was house-proud, neither cared how much washing-up was piled in the sink. Neither of them liked rats so they kept two large tom-cats. They ate meals out of tins and plastic containers and gave what remained to the cats. When they went 'walkabout', which was Eden's name for their sudden journeys to unexpected places, they sometimes stayed in cheap hotels and sometimes slept rough. When they were away the cats menaced the neighbouring colony of drug-dependents on the Roehampton edge of the common. Drug dependents were cared for by the state and provided with their drug allowance on the understanding that they were in rehabilitation. In fact there was very little rehabilitation in the drug colonies. The world movement to make all drugs available at the expense of each individual state, and to rehabilitate all users when they were willing, had been something of a failure. Drug use among Outsiders was on the increase. Insiders, of course, never touched the stuff. Eden had been a user when young. He was no addict but he had been known to wander over to the rehab-compound of an evening and share a joint with one or two of the skeletal creatures who sat outside the battered doors. Prune was never allowed to join him there and she exhibited a healthy disgust towards everything that came under the heading of drugs. She had Piers to thank for that, and in this, as in all things, she knew that he was right.

Prune loved Eden but she idolised Piers. When they had been young men and the family had sometimes foregathered at their father's house, Piers and Eden had played a game that involved taking it in turns to throw a ball in a high arc over the roof from the front of the house, then dashing through to the back and catching the ball before it hit the ground. Both the boys, or men as they seemed to Prune, could do this with ease. It was an exciting event to watch. The masterly throw and then the stampede of masculine strength with the wafted odour of sweat and hair grease and clean shirts. Prune loved them when they played like that, because she saw it happen so rarely. And it was her dearest ambition to throw a ball over the house and catch it on the other side. Not in competition with them, just on her own, for its own sake. She had tried it a few times but she seemed to have floppy wrists that would not throw properly. Even so the ambition remained. Sometimes she tried to do it at Wimbledon but it never worked.

Eden hated Insiders. To him they seemed more likely to be corrupt than any of the Outsiders in the communes. To Prune they were nice people who swept past in big glittering cars and went to the opera and things. Prune did not particularly want to go to the opera but she would have liked to ride in a big, glittery car. She knew that Piers rode in a car like that because she often saw him on television. Sometimes she thought she had chosen to live with the wrong brother. She did not know how completely the choice had been made for her. Sometimes, when Eden was grumpy or they had had a disagreement, she would say,

'I think I'll go and live with Piers.' When she said this Eden would roar with laughter and say,

'Try it, that's all. Just try it!'

Of course Prune never had tried it but she had it in the back of her mind that one day she just might.

3~

Una lived in the uncharted social hinterland between the Insiders and the Outsiders but her lifestyle was nothing like Eden's and Prune's. She had no desire to live among the protected rich, although she had money enough to allow her a lifestyle comparable to theirs. Nor did she seek a place among the shack dwellers and the homeless. Her way of life belonged to another age when farms and small holdings were a natural part of the countryside and those who had a small patch of land could live self-sufficient and contented lives.

Una owned a few acres of land, in the now neglected English countryside between High Wycombe and Reading. She kept chickens and a few goats. She tilled the soil and grew a strict rotation of crops, taking care at which phase of the moon she planted them. Fifty years earlier there had been plenty like her. Now she knew of none. Not that she went searching. She had too much to do at home. If people needed help or advice they came to her. She was respected as a spiritual advisor. She had a reputation among the Outsiders for kindness and they also valued her wisdom. Her produce was also much prized by some of the Insiders who stopped their shiny cars at the little stall she kept set up at the constantly open gate of her property and where she sold seasonable vegetables, eggs, honey and home made jams and chutneys. Her price list for the Insiders was displayed on a blackboard at the side of the stall. People helped themselves and left the money in a box with a slot in the lid. Insiders were scrupulously honest. They cared so much about reputation. Her prices for Outsiders were very much lower. Sometimes, if their need was great, she charged them nothing or asked them to give what they could afford. When Outsiders came to her door they were usually in need. Once, some years ago, one of them made off with the box with the slit in the lid. She didn't phone the police. There was no need. A group of Outsiders soon brought the box and the money back. Her ongoing help to them was too much valued to be exploited or cast aside.

Una's reputation rested in part on her knowledge of herbal medicine. She helped all who came to her in need of this and charged nothing at all. She had watched over recovery, birth and death and treated each as an inevitable part of life.

Her home was unpretentious but full of small pleasures and comforts of her own. In the early days of her life there it had been ransacked so many times that she had learnt to hold on to nothing, to depend on nothing. She kept nothing concealed and never locked her doors and, knowing this, nobody ever robbed her or took advantage of her any more. Only her tool-kit and her best cooking pots really counted with her and she could lock these away in time of need in a large concrete box, sunk in the earth at the edge of the orchard. It was easy to padlock the box and cover it with earth, stones and twigs. She kept the key to this store chest in a secret place. If anyone came to the house in her absence they were welcome to what was there. At the edge of the orchard, and all round the property, the wilderness of nature was just kept at bay. That was how Una liked it.

4~

The Derbyshires were a model family. They lived in a detached period house overlooking parkland not far from the efficiently guarded southern gates of their compound. These gates were close to the area once known as Swiss Cottage and so this main entry to the compound was still known as Swiss Gate, though very few people knew why. The compound was bounded by the main South-North road out of London on its eastern side and by a hill still known as Archway Road to the west, though there was no Archway nowadays to suggest why the road was so named. The north boundary followed exactly the northern edge of Hampstead Heath so that this, together with the park close to Swiss Gate, gave the compound dwellers two large open spaces where they could walk and where their children were safe to play. This made the Hampstead and Highgate compound, known as the H & H, one of the most sought after compounds in London. Only the Chelsea compound with its river frontage was seen as more desirable, though the many guard posts along the river, which had been placed there to avoid the usual high fencing, made residence in The Chelsea very costly indeed. The cleaners, park-keepers and guards in any compound were paid for jointly by the residents and the Compound Council employed the workers and fixed the tariffs and their wages. The workers were low grade Insiders and lived in blocks of flats situated near the compounds where they worked. These flats, like the compounds, were well guarded. Generally speaking, the more expensive it was to live in a compound the better were its services, meaning that the workers who lived in good quality apartments were better paid and tended to be better educated, to have a better lifestyle and to be more willing because they were more contented.

The two Derbyshire children were part of the state Internet Educational Scheme and studied for several days a week at their own computers in their study bedrooms. They also attended a group at the study house near the Heath for three half days a week, which gave them one-to-one contact with a teacher for problem-solving and advice. This also gave them the experience of working as part of a group for subjects such as music and drama and enabled them to socialise with other children in a controlled environment. Teachers in such local study houses had considerable powers. They set up and checked the computer terminals of each of their pupils and maintained a connection with each via a master computer in the study house. They assessed the progress of each child's work and were able, at any given moment, to produce a detailed report as to the child's standards, ability range, intelligence and application. Teachers' reports, and eventually their references and recommendations for employment, were a significant factor in an individual's career advancement. For this reason, teachers were highly valued in society and very well paid.

Benjamin was eleven, still at an age when general studies were compulsory. His curriculum covered maths, science, geography, literature, music, drama, art and history - including the early stages of political history and social psychology. Lucy was fourteen and she was allowed to specialise if she wished. She had opted for a course including biology, literature, and the history of art. The rudiments of art history were included in the group sessions in the earlier general studies, but children with a special aptitude were able to treat it as a specialist subject when they made their pre-career training choices at fourteen. Lucy showed talent and a sensitivity towards all things artistic, a fact that was well disguised by her adolescent determination to hide every vestige of emotion or enthusiasm for anything.

Outsider children were educated in old-fashioned schools left over from the turn of the century. There was much truanting and classes were over-crowded. Outsider teachers were usually Insiders who had seen better days and dropped out for various reasons. It was generally agreed throughout Western countries that an Outsider education fitted an individual for little or nothing that was worthwhile. The Insider internet educational scheme could not be accessed by Outsiders most of whom could not afford their own computer and did not have a pre-paid IES course with a password to give them access to it. Provision was made for use of communal computers, free of charge, at social centres and public libraries, but access was for short periods only and the computers were out-dated cast-offs donated by Insiders and they were too unreliable for sustained internet use, breaking down frequently or being unable to access the newest web sites and programmes.

The Derbyshires kept their children well away from any real knowledge of the world of Outsiders. For this very reason Lucy was becoming fascinated by everything to do with the Outsider world. She had romantic notions of an Outsider falling in love with her and stealing her away to live in thrilling squalor with a delicate amount of violent sex thrown in.

Ben had been studying the old customs of football in his history lessons. The huge gatherings in vast stadia, and the riots that had ensued, before live attendance at football matches had been banned, interested him very much. The stars of football then had been like great actors or famous musicians now. Ben thought he would have loved to go to a football match, even though it was now known that the results of matches were rigged nine times out of ten. Tennis and cricket were played within the compounds, and matches against other compounds were played at home or away, but large crowds were not permitted and the Derbyshires rarely went to such events. Valerie Derbyshire, the children's mother was more interested in theatre than sport and they would all go to the Central London Arts Zone, where only registered compound dwellers could apply for passes, to see plays by the great writers past and present. Valerie believed this was an important aspect of the children's education. Ian preferred the opera and, although the children were often bored with it, they were taken to the great opera houses in the CLAZ from time to time. Ian and Valerie Derbyshire were determined that their children should grow up with all the refinements that Insider life could give them.

5~

The Elite Society was holding a celebration dinner at Pinecott Cedars, the country mansion which was their headquarters. The long dinner table was set up in the old fashioned way with real silver and cut crystal and many branched candlesticks whose slender candles gave off a faint scent of beeswax as well as a gently mysterious light. The table decorations were arranged between the candlesticks and were of cream roses and golden carnations. The Coalport dinner service, on which the courses would be served, was more than two hundred years old. In one corner of the room a string quartet was playing Haydn on a dais surrounded with green ferns and lilies. As the diners assembled there were gasps of awe and delight. It was a setting from a bygone age.

The Elite Society had existed now for a hundred years and this was their centenary celebration. The members, all men, had been allowed to bring their wives tonight, because of the uniqueness of the occasion. Normally the men met and dined without female companions. The members were all politicians, lawyers, business tycoons and, occasionally, very high ranking civil servants and heads of major public schools. Election was by invitation on the recommendation of no fewer than four existing members. Prime Ministers, Chancellors and Speakers of the House of Commons had been among its members in the past. No one knew what was discussed at the monthly meetings of the ES, in fact the general population hardly knew of their existence. Those who did know were either dismissive or derogatory unless they were among the few who hoped one day to be included in the membership. It was said in some quarters that politicians rose and fell according to their standing with the ES.

Hugo Finch and his wife Isabel were guests of honour on this occasion. Hugo was a member of parliament in the coalition government led by the new Prime Minister, Sebastian Drew. He had fallen out with Drew when they were both backbenchers and had, predictably, not been offered a place in the cabinet. The Elitists, however, had higher aspirations for him. There had never been a member of the Elite Society elected to the World Parliament. There had been several attempts to get members accepted but without success. Hugo seemed to be the perfect candidate to succeed. He was suave, handsome, educated and one of the most brilliant members of the English bar. He would have to give up much of his legal practice of course and resign from the House of Commons, but these would be small sacrifices in comparison to becoming a member of Piers Diamond's government.

Election to the World Parliament was controlled by a Council of Electors, one from each nation. This huge body was in itself chosen with extreme care from among those with an impeccable record, an assured income, and who had risen to a position in life that ensured they were beyond political or professional ambition. Many of the electors were elderly. Membership of the Council was for the remainder of the man or woman's useful life and no payment other than expenses was ever made to them. Many famous names were to be found on the Council. Members might never be approached or canvassed in any way by a person seeking election to the World Parliament, nor by any agent on their behalf, modern technology being such that this could never occur without its being discovered.

Isabel, as the wife of the guest of honour, was seated on the right of the president, Sir Anthony Partridge, who was at the head of the table. Hugo was next to Isabel. Doctor Paul Ramsey, the headmaster of Eton with his wife Anthea sat opposite and next to them Ian and Valerie Derbyshire, the society's treasurer and his wife. On Hugo's right was the wife of the Chief Whip and her husband was next to her. The president chatted almost flirtatiously with Isabel during the soup and fish courses. When the meat course was served he announced to the company,

'Here you have a delicacy costing more than you can imagine. I wish you all bon appetit.'

'It looks wonderful,' said Isabel Finch, picking up her knife and fork delicately. The two little rolls of meat on her plate were carefully encased in puff pastry, decoratively on either side were five perfect asparagus tips and this attractive dish was completed by thinly sliced potatoes in a cheese and herb sauce. Neither the delicately flavoured soup nor the rolls of smoked salmon and cream cheese of the previous courses had destroyed Isabel's considerable appetite. She speared one of the puff pastry rolls with her fork and it oozed in a wonderfully aromatic way. Her knife went through it so lightly it might have been made of foam. Hugo was watching her as she took her first mouthful.

'What do you think of that?' asked the president.

'Mmm,' said Isabel, luxuriating in the taste, 'this is heavenly. What is it?'

'Something very special that we reserve for important occasions.'

'I think it's sucking pig or very tender veal,' Isabel said, taking another mouthful.

'Well. . .' said Hugo, but the president interrupted him.

'Don't tell her. Let her guess.'

'I wasn't going to . . .'

'I think it must be pork,' said Anthea Ramsey across the table, 'It has that flavour of pork, but only very faintly. I'm afraid I think it's probably very young sucking-pig. Oh, let's not think about it.'

'I hope there are no Jews here,' said Valerie Derbyshire. 'They might not like to eat this without being told what it is and there seems to be no printed menu.'

'There are no Jews here,' said Hugo. They looked down the length of the table at the other guests. Expletives of delight were to be heard above the general buzz of conversation.

'Couldn't you afford a menu?' joked Valerie, 'I think it would have been nice.'

'I think it's better to let the food speak for itself,' said her husband.

'There speaks our frugal treasurer,' said the president.

'The new chef seems to be a success,' said Hugo.

'Yes, he ought to be.' said the president. 'He's costing us an arm and a leg. Isn't he, Ian?'

'I'm afraid so,' said Ian.

'Oh, dear! Not yours I hope,' said Paul Ramsey. 'If it's your arm or leg we're eating I'll skip the rest of this course.'

'Don't be disgusting,' said his wife.

'Sorry,' he smiled at the president, 'That's what comes of being exposed to school-boy humour for half a lifetime. One eventually becomes indoctrinated. Anyway, Anthea, one of his legs would be a lot tougher than this.'

'Not in very good taste,' said Hugo, glaring at him.

'Unlike the food,' said the headmaster's wife.

'I think Paul was trying to put the ladies off their dinner,' said the president.

'You won't do that,' said Isabel. Her plate was nearly clean already.

'Slow down, darling,' said Hugo in her ear. 'You'll give yourself indigestion.'

After a pavlova and a sorbet and a wonderful array of cheeses, all accompanied by several very fine wines, coffee was served and the president rose to his feet.

'Ladies and gentlemen,' he said, 'and may I say what a pleasure it is to have ladies with us tonight. I am sure that all ES members are aware of a refinement that is attributable to their presence.' There were murmurs of agreement from several of the members. The president continued,

'My first duty tonight is to propose a toast to the society itself. We have been in existence for one hundred years today and I like to believe that we, the present membership, continue the good work of our forbears. ES money has gone towards the improvement of education, health and higher social standards throughout this precious and beautiful land of ours. We have upheld the slogans 'England for the English' and 'Britain for the British' with a fervour that would make our grandfathers proud. We have continued to make our mark. We have upheld what is best in all aspects of educated living. I give you, ladies and gentlemen, the Elite Society and long may it continue.' The company rose and 'The Elite Society' was uttered in many and varied tones. They drank and sat down again. The president continued. 'I have seen many fine men come and go during my membership of the Society. None finer than Hugo Finch. He is a man well known to us all and I will not embarrass him by extolling his many virtues. Suffice it to say that he is, to my mind, underrated - undervalued even - in this country of ours at the present time.' Several murmurs of 'Very true' and 'Shame!'. The president lifted his head as if braving a storm. 'We however do not undervalue him. We see him for what he is. A loyal member and an exceptional human being. It is, as many of you know, our intention to put his name forward for election to the World Parliament. The Chief Whip will endorse our recommendation and I have no doubt that Hugo will come through the lengthy selection process via the Council of Electors with flying colours. As we all know the mills of God grind slowly, but not nearly as slowly as those of the Council of Electors.' A general murmur of laughter followed here. Gratified that the assembled company was with him in spirit, the president continued, 'Nevertheless I hope that by this time next year we shall be able to congratulate our special member of the World Parliament. It is long overdue that one of our number should have the influence that such a position brings. In anticipation of his success I give you Hugo Finch!' The toast was drunk enthusiastically and everyone sat down again. There were one or two shouts of 'Speech!' and Hugo got up and, with charming reluctance, said the few words that he had been rehearsing in front of Isabel every evening for the last week.

When they got home in the early hours and were comfortably side by side in bed he asked Isabel if the speech had been alright. There was no reply. Isabel was already fast asleep.

6~

Isabel pulled the car over into the slow lane and turned off into the tree-lined road that led to Una's place. After nearly half a mile she pulled off the side road into Una's lane and parked her car on a stretch of tyre-marked grass among the trees, a few yards from the sagging wooden gate that was propped open with a pile of old bricks. She was not going to risk her beautifully tuned engine to the ruts and pot-holes of Una's neglected driveway.

Another car, rather a muddy and battered looking car, was parked on the road side beyond the gate. A man was sitting in the driving seat. Isabel did not like to stare at him but she guessed he was an Outsider. One of those people Una still insisted on associating with in the name of social conscience. It was a pleasant walk along the grass under the trees beside the drive. As she came in sight of the house a small figure passed her. It was an abnormally short girl with a bouncy and determined walk and a round, slightly vacant face. Isabel recognised the sort of disability she had heard described in relation to past times when medicine was more primitive. She felt a slight shudder as the child went by. After a couple of hundred yards Isabel came up to the house and saw Una coming round the corner with a basket of eggs and a large bunch of carrots.

'Hello!' Isabel called, 'I hope this isn't a bad time?'

Una set down the basket and bunch of carrots near the door and, wiping her hands on her skirt, came to Isabel and embraced her. She smelt of earth with a background of fragrant soap.

'There's no such thing as a bad time here,' she said. 'Come in, I'll make some tea.'

'Who on earth was that?' said Isabel as they went indoors.

'Who do you mean?'

'That odd little person I passed in the drive.'

'That was Prunella, my goddaughter. She's been staying with me for a few days.'

'But she's … I mean she's not normal.'

'She was born with Down's Syndrome, that's all.'

'That's all? - Poor child! I though they'd stamped that out.'

They sat down at the scrubbed kitchen table and Una set the kettle to boil on the stove.

'I felt I needed to see you,' Isabel said.

'It's been a long time.'

'I know. And now it looks as if we might be moving to Switzerland.'

'Really?'

'Yes. Not giving up our place here, of course, but setting up a home there too because Hugo's applying for membership of the World Parliament.'

'You sound pretty certain he'll be successful.'

'Well, you know Hugo. He gets what he wants'

'How do you feel about that?'

'I think it will be wonderful.'

'You sound as if it's all settled.'

'Well, he's being recommended by all the members of the Elite Society and several MPs in addition, I think. I don't see how the recommendation can fail.'

'Has a member of the Elite Society ever been accepted by the Council of Electors before?'

'No, I don't think so. That's why it's very important that Hugo succeeds. Everyone was so keen about it at the ES dinner the other night. Hugo is so impressive. They can't turn him down. It would be like a sort of ongoing prejudice against the ES, wouldn't it?'

'As I understand it the ES is not without its prejudices.'

'They just think national characteristics should be kept pure.'

'British characteristics, I take it you mean.'

'So, what's wrong with that?'

'It sounds a bit like the Nazi Party of old.'

'I don't think Hugo would agree with you at all.'

'Wasn't Hugo at school with the First Minister?'

'Yes, and they hated each other. But that's all in the past. Piers Diamond couldn't be petty enough to block Hugo's appointment just because they didn't get on at school.'

'That could depend on why they didn't get on.' Una was bringing two mugs of herbal tea to the table. 'You don't mind elderflower tea, I hope?'

'Anything will do,' said Isabel.

'Have a cookie,' Una said, as she fetched a plate of them from the dresser. The cookies looked quite delicious, all buttery with crumbly edges. Isabel took one eagerly. 'Prunella and I made them this morning,' said Una. Isabel put the cookie down at once and looked at it suspiciously.

'You were a friend of Piers Diamond's mother, weren't you?' she said.

'Of his stepmother, yes. That is why I'm Prunella's godmother. Prunella was her last child. She died soon after the birth. I was with her. She asked me to be Prunella's godmother then and I feel a special responsibility. A special privilege too. Prune is a very dear person.' Isabel, unable to resist the crumbly edge, picked up the biscuit and dunked it in her tea. The edge crumbled and fell off before she could get it to her mouth.

'They're very fresh, the biscuits. If you dunk that you may lose most of it in your tea,' Una said, smiling. Isabel took a bite of undunked biscuit. It was delicious.

'You must have got to know Piers pretty well when he was younger, being such a close friend of his family,' she said.

'I never saw much of him then,' Una was always unforthcoming on the subject of Piers.

'And now?'

'He visits me very occasionally, if he has a free moment when he's in this country, which happens very rarely.'

'He's over here now.'

'Is he?'

'You must know he is. It's been on all the news programmes.'

'I don't watch television. I have too much to do.'

'Well, now I've told you he's here, do you expect to see him?'

'I never expect to see him, Isabel. He's a very busy man and I too have a very full life. I doubt very much . . .'

'But you could talk to him on your phone - or mail him on the net.'

'It's not something I ever do.'

'Una - please - I'm asking for your help.'

'Isabel, this is not the sort of help I give people.'

'Please - for Hugo's sake.'

'No, Isabel. I can't help you and you know very well that I can't. What's more I wouldn't even if I could. Piers has his advisors. He makes his own decisions. I couldn't possibly presume to raise a topic like this.'

'You don't like Hugo much, do you?'

'Is that a rhetorical question?'

'You don't like him. I know you don't.'

'I will say this, Isabel, I don't much like the Elite Society. The whole idea is anathema to me and I honestly believe that if membership of such a society could influence the First Minister or the Council of Electors the world government would be in a bad way.'

'But why?'

'Because elitism encourages the divisions in society. I believe it could lead to even greater divisions than we have already.'

'What do you mean?'

'Well, think about it for a moment. Are any Outsiders included in the membership of the ES?'

'No, of course not!'

'What about Jews?'

'None that I know.'

'Blacks? Asians - or half-Asians like Piers?'

'I - don't think so,' Isabel finished her cookie.

'Are you happy about that?'

'I don't know any Jews. I don't know any Outsiders, for that matter.'

'I'm an Outsider, Isabel.' She pushed the plate of cookies towards Isabel who took another.

'You're not an Outsider!' she said, 'You're a highly educated and very clever woman who has, from time to time, the ear of the First Minister of the World Parliament. You're nothing like an Outsider, any more than he is.'

'I am what I am and Hugo is what he is and we must stand or fall by that.'

'You don't think Hugo will succeed.'

'I'm not a fortune-teller, Isabel.' Una opened her work-grimed hands on the table and Isabel looked down at her own perfectly manicured fingers which were decorated with rings. She gave a pathetic little sniff.

'I'm disappointed in you,' she said, taking a lace handkerchief out of her handbag and dabbing her eyes with it very carefully so as not to disturb her mascara, 'I thought our friendship was worth more than that. I'm only asking a small favour.'

'That would not come under the heading of what I call a small favour,' said Una. 'Piers is a man of huge integrity and to attempt to sway him in relation to anything as dubious as the Elite Society would not only taint my relationship with him, it would lead him to see Hugo through my eyes as a suitable candidate for membership of the world government and that is contrary to what I believe.'

Isabel got up.

'I'm going now,' she said coldly. 'Thank you for the tea and the cookies.'

'Take a few with you,' said Una. Isabel softened. She hesitated. The cookies were really marvellous.

'Oh, may I?'

'Of course.' Una produced a crumpled paper bag and tipped the rest of the plateful of cookies into it. 'There!'

'Thank you so much!' Isabel moved round the table and gave her a peck on the cheek. They did not hug each other.

Driving home in her glistening vehicle Isabel went over and over her conversation with Una and felt discomforted. What was it they had said at the ES dinner? 'You won't find any Jews here.' Was Hugo prejudiced? Was the Elite Society a reincarnated National Front or Nazi organisation of the kind that all countries had long ago agreed to stamp out under the influence of the World Parliament? If the ES was really fostering racism, Hugo hadn't a hope in hell of being elected. Well, she shrugged her tense shoulders and relaxed back in her seat, she had tried. She had done her best and, if nothing came of it, Hugo need never know that she had been to see Una. She was not to blame.

7~

Piers Diamond had always been a loner. In fact, it could be said that he had always seen himself as profoundly alone. His younger half-brother and very much younger sister had never seemed to have much in common with him and, although he was fond of them, he had not grown up with a sentimental attachment to his family and he had no such attachment to the memory of his parents. These facts had given him a freedom and knowledge of himself from an early age such as few people ever experience. Even in childhood he had been blessed with the kind of intelligence adults respect. He had been head-boy at his school and then head of various committees and debating societies at Oxford, where he had eventually shone as a leading member of the Union. His degree in philosophy and politics was the highest the university awarded in his year and his eventual doctoral thesis became a best-seller in political circles across the world and the five succinct works that followed it were even more successful. It was as if he had always been destined to become First Minister of the World Parliament. And so, at forty-two years of age, this was his role on the world stage.

In the decades prior to his premiership the gradually developing World Parliament had achieved much that ensured global peace and the security of the planet, and a great deal of this had been based on his own early writings, which were now standard instruction for the running of a safe and peaceful world society in an un-endangered environment. Equality of trade had only been a beginning. National armies and stockpiles of weapons had been disbanded in favour of a world peace-keeping force that moved in with the minimum of blood-shed on any country contravening the established laws of peace and respect for life. Transport had been revolutionised and all vehicles were either battery operated or powered by hydrogen. The land loss that had resulted from the sea's encroachment as a result of earlier global warming had now been halted completely. The planet was stable. Solar energy, carbon capture and storage and hydro electric power had been developed to a degree of refinement never imagined in the days when humanity had so haphazardly tried to side-step the threatening build up of carbon emissions. The ozone layer had been, if not repaired, at least strengthened by positive chemical emissions which ensured prevention of further damage. Factory Farming had been abandoned and was now a criminal offence. More than half the world's population was now vegetarian and the vast amounts of grain once used to feed cattle were now available to feed countries whose populations had once suffered from poor nutrition. Society was wiser and more responsible on a world scale, and when lapses occurred, action was quickly taken to restore the equilibrium.

Piers was a man of huge integrity. He was quietly spoken but his speech had a kind of considered authority which made people listen to him. He gave himself no airs and graces. He was a man who seemed always to be considering with care and responsibility how to act for the best. He respected all beings and, because his respect was evident to all, he won the respect of all in response.

Walking to the World Parliament building on his return to Geneva, with his security team close and vigilant around him, Piers found his mind dwelling on the range of world problems that continued to trouble him. One of the foremost of these was the problem of inequality. In almost every country the division between the Insiders and the Outsiders was becoming increasingly marked and this was unacceptable. Responsible citizens the world over were now living in a state of improved health and safety. But Piers was aware that 'responsible citizens' was, in any Western country, a term synonymous with 'wealthy citizens'. His plans, his writings and his statesmanship had never in any sense recommended wealth as a passport to privilege. Nevertheless, in most Western countries, the rich now lived in large houses, situated in spacious compounds with guards at the gates whilst those who could not afford such housing lived in places that were badly maintained and totally unprotected. National governments were, in the main, allowing Outsider properties to become increasingly derelict. It was often stated as an excuse that Outsiders lived as they wanted to live and could have maintained their properties if they wished. In most Western countries government grants were available. It seemed however that more and more Outsiders were living rough and getting by on their wits. It had been the dream of Piers' heart to eliminate crime and poverty from the earth. India, Africa, The Middle East and China were becoming richer and more stable every year under the new fair trading laws. But in Europe, America and Britain, the home where he had grown up and been educated, an element of society seemed to have elected to live in a degree of poverty that they called the New Freedom, a condition which Piers was beginning to recognise as increasingly dangerous. Britain and India were in fact the countries with the strictest class divides. It seemed ironic to Piers that the two lands that had been responsible for the very blood in his veins were the two most reluctant to show the social unity and tolerance that he believed in.

Many aspects of Western society were praiseworthy. Longevity was a direct result of the improvements in spending on health and science by the World Government. The rising numbers of people reaching their hundredth birthday was a credit to modern science. There was now a strictly controlled birth-rate. The maximum of two children (the simple adult replacement plan) had become a rule in all countries. Piers knew, as did all members of the World Parliament, that there were certain cases where illegal trading took place in relation to child numbers. Childless couples had increasingly begun to sell all or part of their child allocation to those who sought larger families. These 'extra' children would then be registered in the name of the childless whilst being brought up in the extended families who had paid for the right to give birth to them as extras. This was not at the present time illegal. Piers was not sure whether to bow to a pressure group in the World Parliament and allow a law to come into force to make it illegal or whether to let a little lee-way remain. There were other pressing matters at stake. The Council of Electors was considering the recommendation of several new members for the parliament and he had grave doubts about one of these. The World Parliament had never been divided into parties. Representatives of all nations sat together as a coalition of equals in the great parliament building in Geneva. Party politics had almost disappeared from the earth. Following the example of Geneva, most countries were governed by a coalition in which the members sought for the national good rather than for the advancement of their own parties. Many countries also had a second house of Electors to vet those recommended for parliamentary service and to curb the parliament if it became unduly biased or extreme in its policies. The Council of Electors at Geneva was a body of people of very great integrity. They scrutinised every recommendation to the World Parliament and it was only with the full agreement of the Council that a member was accepted. The Electors themselves were many and varied. They were selected for their skill and integrity and they did an excellent job. Even so, on occasion, Piers had found himself at odds with their decisions. He had a strong but not an absolute power of veto. He was unsure at this juncture whether he should call it into play at this time. He did not believe that Hugo Finch was a suitable candidate for a seat at Geneva. Turning these thoughts over in his mind Piers walked through the sunshine towards the parliament building and the bodyguards, their hands on their hidden guns and their eyes discreetly scanning their surroundings, accompanied him.

8~

Julia had been feeling ill for several days. She had let her friend Patches, and one or two other boys who favoured mescaline, persuade her to join them for a session and the drug seemed to have got her in the guts. She was used to cannabis. She liked the feeling of lightness and fun it reliably gave her. She often behaved in a very silly way after sharing a joint. She never smoked on her own. She wasn't interested in nicotine and she wasn't interested in anything addictive, but life in the commune was often very depressing and the kind of work that was available was equally so. She did some erratic cleaning and counter serving at a local battery exchange station. This enhanced her state allowance and enabled her to get by but she was often very low and couldn't be bothered to go to work. The battery station manager was pretty understanding but he sometimes yelled at her. The mescaline had seemed like a fun idea. Mescaline, like pot, was cheap and available on demand at the drug centres. No one made money out of dealing drugs, the state had taken all that over long ago. Addicts got their doses free and were encouraged onto rehabilitation programmes at the state's expense. Outsiders were not forced to give up their drugs. Only alcohol and nicotine were discouraged and, since they were extremely costly and seen as old-fashioned, few Outsiders had much interest in them. The supplied drugs were preferable. Alcohol was an expensive luxury enjoyed by Insiders from time to time. Drunkenness was unpopular for its crassness, and the huge cost it represented debarred Outsiders from considering it.

The mescaline had been better by far than pot. Julia had felt she could fly. When she woke the next morning and staggered out of bed to retch for an hour or more she began to wonder if it had been such a good idea. The retching returned next day and the day after. She lay in bed feeling exhausted and afraid to eat. Eventually someone suggested that she ought to go and see Una.

The long tree-lined drive was almost the last straw. The train journey had been arduous and it had been a long walk from the station. The countryside outside London looked to Julia empty rather than attractive. Fields and woods were not her thing and they were unkempt except for the verges at the roadside. She had been told where Una lived but it had not been easy to find. This was probably the longest walk she had taken in her life and she had eaten next to nothing for three days and was almost at fainting point when she reached the door. There was a hanging iron bell in the porch with a chain attached to the clapper. She pulled it and the bell swung to and fro with an ear-splitting sound. Almost at once Una opened the door. She looked homely and alert with a face that might have been beautiful before she neglected her looks for more important things. Julia said,

'I seem to have got ill. Can you help me, please?'

'Come in,' said Una. She spoke warmly and Julia swayed against the post of the porch. It seemed as if the last effort of toiling up the drive had been all she could manage. 'Steady,' said Una and took her arm and helped her to a chair by the fire.

It took nearly a week of careful diet, gentle exercise and plenty of sleep before Una would contemplate letting Julia go back to the commune. By the time she was ready for the return journey Julia knew that she was probably pregnant. Una had found out quite a lot about her in the intervening days. She knew that Julia had no partner and that she cared for hardly anyone in the commune, apart from a young drug-addict whom she called Patches. Julia seemed to want to go back to make sure that Patches was all right. She described his struggle against addiction and it was obvious that she was intent on helping him. It was also obvious from all that Julia said that Patches was not the father of her child. If Julia knew who the father was, she was certainly not willing to name him. Una took her back to the commune in her own battered vehicle. She had made Julia promise that she would go to the nearest hospital with a free maternity clinic and Julia, having come to trust Una, had agreed to do so. Even so, it was several days before she plucked up the courage to go for a pregnancy test.

9~

Hugo was working his way through a pile of newspapers. He took all the main daily papers and carefully scoured them for information that might be useful to him. Hugo had many enemies, at least that is how he saw them. The enemies themselves usually had no idea that they were on Hugo's 'hit list' or that he imagined himself to be on theirs. Hugo was a bitter man. At school he had been a bitter boy, always disappointed, always believing that he could have shone if it had not been for this or that brilliant charlatan who was deliberately and cleverly doing him down. His worst enemy at that time had been Piers Diamond. He had never forgiven Piers for his brilliance and success. As this success had grown, and Piers' exalted position in the world had become impossible to ignore, Hugo had grown more and more resentful. Piers was the very opposite of himself and Hugo hated the thought of him. This did not stop him avidly reading every word about him that appeared in the press. He turned over a page of the Times and discovered a half page close-up of his enemy.

'Bloody Piers again!'

'Don't read about him if it upsets you so much.' His wife wanted a trouble-free existence. She became very easily irritated by Hugo's pointless vitriol.

'Please shut up, Isabel. I need someone to hate. You know that. It gives me a sense of purpose.'

'I don't see how anyone can hate Piers Diamond. He's about the most brilliant statesman history has ever recorded and the world's a better place for his ideas and policies. What do you want? Wars? Planetary disintegration? He's taken all that on practically single-handed, and all you can do is scoff at him. Just take a realistic look at his policies, most of them are wonderful. You can't possibly imagine that you, with all this hate inside you, could have done a better job.'

'The man's a prig. Most of his "wonderful policies" were probably stolen from someone else. He has teams of scientists working for him, feeding him information, and then he claims their ideas as his own.'

'Of course he has advisors, any statesman does, but you can't say he takes all the credit. We all know who his scientific advisors are. He's completely open about that. It's one of his strengths that he's not afraid to take informed advice.'

'If he dropped dead tomorrow it would make very little difference to world government. In fact, it would be a huge improvement.'

'You only say that because you're afraid he'll block you from getting your place in the World Parliament.'

'If he does I think I'll assassinate the bastard.'

'You are joking, I hope.'

'Of course I am, but Gandhi was assassinated, Martin Luther King, John Kennedy. They were really good men. Why doesn't somebody bump off this little shit? I'd like to do it. I'd really love to!'

'I sometimes wonder what I'm doing here, married to you, when you're capable of saying things like that. You have such a nasty mind.'

'I suppose I have a devious mind. I always did have. At school I used to steal Diamond's rough notes from his waste paper basket and make a précis of his work to get high marks for myself. Once I stole a letter he'd written to a girl.'

'Did you copy that too?'

'No, but I told the girl a few things about him that put her out of his reach.'

'True things?'

'No - lies. It was very satisfying. I watched their little drama from a distance. It was a good time. I enjoyed it. I loved the power.'

'Did he find out?'

'Never. I think the crap-head actually thought I admired him when I hung around.'

'In a way you do. At least you're obsessed with him.'

'I'm not!'

'Oh, yes. You've never been as fascinated by anyone as you are by Piers Diamond.'

'Well, now he's the one with the power. His single voice could deny me a seat in the World Parliament, no matter how many people recommend me. It's unbearable to know that. I've never wanted anything as much as I want this.'

'Be patient, darling, you usually get what you want.'

10~

Julia came out of the clinic with a damp tissue paper towel screwed up in a ball in her hand. She had cried when the doctor had given her the news. She did not intend to cry again in the road and arrive home with red eyes and a swollen face and have everyone ask what was the matter. She had not meant to get pregnant. She had firmly believed she had no desire for a baby and never would have. But something was growing inside her that could not be ignored and some part of herself, deep down and almost unrecognisable, had begun to flicker in wonder at the sense of a new life beginning. A life for which she was responsible, however unintentionally.

Julia lived in a commune with a shifting population of some twenty Outsiders. Many of them were on drugs. They were legitimate users with doctors' prescriptions for their doses and they attended the local drug-users' clinic regularly in accordance with the law. Julia had never been interested in drugs, with the exception of the occasional joint. The few times she had tried anything heavier she had been so sick and had such a headache afterwards that she had decided not to repeat the experience. But she was often depressed and sometimes lonely. On such occasions she usually ended up in bed with one of the men in the commune. It was a way of convincing herself that she mattered or that someone cared. She had no idea who was the father of her child. In many ways she preferred not to know. That way she was spared the heartache of trying to force an unwilling and possibly irresponsible partner to share the responsibility with her. As things were she would have the child all to herself. She would be the only influence in its early life. She would have to find a place to live on her own, away from the commune, and she would have to manage without leaning on anyone else or blaming them when things were hard. But things had started to get hard already, much harder than she had expected. In the huge and over-stretched public hospital, attended by all the local Outsiders, she had been informed by a rushed and preoccupied doctor that she was carrying a Down's Syndrome foetus and had been strongly advised to have a termination. The word baby had not been used.

She approached the main entrance of the commune slowly. The kicked and peeling paint, the graffiti, the roll-up fag ends littering the pathway all made her feel more miserable than ever. What sort of place was this for a kid to play? She imagined a little moon faced Down's Syndrome child in beautifully clean clothes trotting about among the filth. No, she said to herself. I can't go on living here. She stuffed the screwed up tissue into her pocket and searched for her swipe card. A man came out of the building at that moment and almost collided with her. He was smartly dressed and prosperous looking with clean shoes and leather gloves. He was certainly not an Outsider.

'I beg your pardon,' he said, 'I was looking for someone.'

'Well, I'm Julia. Who do you want?' She looked up at his slightly over-warm and friendly smile and felt afraid.

'You'll do, Julia. You'll do very well. Is there somewhere we could talk - in private?'

'No,' said Julia, 'Out here is as private as it gets.'

'I see,' he said tolerantly, 'Perhaps we could find a quiet corner over there then.'

'Yes, which way do you fancy? The dustbins or the alley where the junkies piss and throw up?' She cringed even as she said the words. She always seemed to have to talk like this to Insiders, as if hitting them over the head with Outsider conditions could change anything.

'We might walk down the road a little way,' he said kindly.

'If you like.' Julia shrugged. They walked away from the building and onto the pavement beside the main traffic flow. After about a hundred yards they came to a small area between the buildings, just opposite the rehabilitation unit. Rehabilitation! That was a joke. Nothing much ever resulted from going there. In the scrubby area between the buildings, grass was struggling to survive around some once brightly painted but now rusting oil drums. It was an area favoured by Outsider children. A see-saw had been made by fixing a battered plank over one of the drums. There was a good deal of litter about. The collectors came once a month and took street rubbish to the trash pits. They were due in a day or two. The man slowed his stride and Julia wandered slowly towards the oil drums and sat down on one of them.

'Not the sort of place where you'd want your child to play,' the man said.

'How do you know about my child?'

'I didn't know. It was just an observation. Tell me about your child.'

'I'm pregnant. I've just learnt this morning that the baby has Down's Syndrome. I've been offered an abortion.'

'That's terrible!' he said.

'I don't know why I told you that.' Julia got out her damp ball of tissue and dabbed her eyes.

'Here,' said the man, producing a perfectly laundered handkerchief from his pocket. For some reason inexplicable to herself, Julia took the handkerchief. She opened it out, blew her nose into the middle of it and then mopped her face. The handkerchief was lovely, soft and smooth with a faint smell of its fresh laundering. Because of that smell Julia was suddenly unable to stop the tears and they began to pour down her face unchecked. The man stood near her but made no move towards her. She continued to sob for several minutes, then, having blown her nose and dried her eyes for one last time, held out the handkerchief to him.

'You must think me very stupid,' she said.

'Not at all,' he answered and then, pushing her arm away gently, 'Do, please, keep the handkerchief.'

'Thanks' said Julia lamely and, after another dab at her eyes, put it in her pocket.

'You need to get away from here,' said the man.

'If only that were possible,' said Julia.

'I might be able to help you.'

'How?'

'There is a house in a London compound. A nice little house. You would have nursing care and your child would be born in comfort.'

'Are you mad? I have no money for that sort of thing. You don't understand this world. You're just slumming. I live here.'

'You need not live here.'

'Some of us don't have your kind of choices.'

'Julia - there are people who need babies. Your baby could make some other people very happy. If you would go to full term with it and let me make all the arrangements I would see to it that you had the means to live in the compound, comfortable and protected with a house and an income for the rest of your life.'

'Why?'

'It's something I do. Some people need babies, other people need a step up in the world. I bring the two factions together when I can. What's wrong with that?'

'I don't know.'

'What don't you know?'

'Something seems wrong. My child won't be normal. It won't be normal. It has Down's Syndrome.'

'Down's Syndrome children are often very sturdy and appealing little people. Your sacrifice will be very much appreciated. You will be more than adequately compensated, I promise you.'

'Why couldn't I live in this house you're offering and bring up my child there?'

'Julia, you must realise that as an unmarried mother you would be unacceptable in a compound.'

'I'd be unacceptable in a compound in any case.'

'Not necessarily. With the right hairdresser and some new clothes, I think there would be a very good case for your full acceptance.'

'But what about the child? I could afford to keep my baby if I had enough money to live in a compound.'

'Your living in a compound is dependent upon your giving up the child. If you keep the child you stay here. If you agree to give it up - if you sign the papers and put yourself into my hands - you will be given a place among Insiders. But only on those terms.'

'I can't do it.'

'Would you like to think about it?'

'No - I can't - I won't do it.'

'As you wish. I'll walk you back to your residence.'

'There's no need.'

'I insist.'

They walked back quickly, Julia keeping a pace ahead of him all the way. As they approached the door and she scrabbled for her swipe, two men came out of the building. One, wearing a threadbare, patched coat, was swaying slightly, the other was holding him up. They were sharing a joint and both looked filthy. Julia stopped with her card in her hand. She did not look at the man although they had already commented on her companion with a degree of mockery. The man made no response to their rudeness and Julia waited for them to go out of hearing.

'I'll do it,' she said suddenly.

'I'm so glad,' he said. 'I'm sure you're making the right decision. I'll ring you.' She took her phone out of her pocket and handed it to him. He transferred its number to his own and returned it to her. 'You could do with a new one,' he said. She didn't answer. She put the phone in her pocket and went inside without looking back. The hallway stank of piss.

11~

'We're going to be living rough for a bit,' Eden said. He said it quite casually, whilst extracting a far from clean spoon from under some plates in the sink. Prune was delighted.

The first thing that happened after this announcement was that he had the phone cut off. This was not unusual. The phone was often cut off because Eden forgot to pay the bill. Getting it put on again was usually expensive and Prune always paid. This was a little unjust as she hardly had any reason to use the phone. She knew almost no one and was uneasy in any case about calling anyone she did not know well. She liked to be able to see a person's face when she was talking to them. The only person she didn't mind phoning was Una.

Next Eden rubbed out their names which had been written in chalk on the wall by the door bell and put 'Gone away,' in scrawled letters. Prior to this he did several very odd things. He packed a lot of papers and a change of clothes into two boxes and took them to the nearest railway station where he put them in a locker. Then he had a copy made of the key the station people had given him and put it on Prune's key-ring with the door key and the key to the bicycle lock, saying,

'This is so that you can get everything back if anything happens to me and you find yourself on your own.'

'Where would you be if I found myself on my own?' asked Prune.

'Probably here - possibly somewhere else,' he said.

'But where?'

'With Una, I suppose.'

'Are you plannin' to go away, then?'

'No.'

'Then why have you given me these keys?'

'Just in case.

'In case of what?'

'In case you find yourself on your own. Now, shut up!'

'But I don't want to be left on my. . . '

'I said, shut up!'

'Yes, but . . .'

'Shut up, Prune, or I'll wallop you.'

12~

Valerie Derbyshire opened the door of her husband's study and put her head in.

'Lucy and Ben are going now,' she said. 'Grandma and Grandpa are ready to take them. Are you coming to say goodbye?'

'Yes, I'll be there in a minute.' Ian began gathering the papers from his desk, moving quickly to cover up the most recent sheet of the Elite Society's accounts which was still in the output tray of the printer.

'Don't keep everyone waiting,' Valerie said.

'I won't!' He spoke tetchily. He did not take kindly to being nagged. Valerie withdrew and he took the accounts sheet, the membership list and some other papers connected with his own investment company and put them in the safe in the wall above the mantelpiece. He closed the door of the safe, letting the combination lock engage, and swung the Picasso print that concealed it into its accustomed place.

The children were in the hall with their luggage explaining to their grandfather which items had to travel in the car with them and which could be put in the boot. Lucy who was fourteen, wanted a large inflatable dolphin in the car with her. She had swum with dolphins on holiday with a friend a few months before and was still enchanted by the memory of this. Ben, who was eleven, and had been jealous of the dolphin trip, was tired of hearing her eulogising about it and was now telling her that she was stupid to take anything so bulky as the dolphin when they were only going to be away for a week. Lucy was insisting that she couldn't be parted from her dolphin and Ben was getting heated and threatening to deflate it with the pin of his sports badge if he had to sit next to it. Valerie was trying to restore peace. The good-natured grandparents were smiling affectionately. They were used to the children. They lived in a compound in Sussex and took the children there two or three times a year. The London compound where Lucy and Ben lived with their parents was larger and more heavily guarded than their grandparents' one. They always felt they were going to the country when they went to Sussex, despite the fact that both compounds had armed guards at the gates and high perimeter fences.

'Come on, guys,' said Ian, 'get on with it if you're going. No one is going to deflate your dolphin, Lucy, or if they do they'll have me to deal with. Okay, young man?'

He came to Ben and ruffled his hair.

'Okay,' said Ben rather reluctantly.

'Real!' said Lucy. This was her favourite word of approval.

'Are we going to get this stuff in the car, then?' said their grandfather.

'Come on,' said Ian, hoisting Lucy's holdall onto his shoulder and picking up Ben's sports bag.'

'Let me pack my own stuff!' shouted Ben.

'All right!' said his father, dropping the sports bag. Lucy ran to the car hugging the dolphin and put it on the back seat. Luggage was stowed and the children and their grandparents got in.

'I told you, I'm not sitting next to that thing!' said Ben, punching the dolphin.

'Oh, shut up!' said Lucy, moving it to the other side of her.

'I wish you joy of them,' said Ian to his parents-in-law.

'They'll be fine,' said their grandmother, smiling at them fondly.

'Goodbye, darlings,' said Valerie, 'be good. Do what Grandma and Grandpa tell you.'

'Yes,' chorused the children in bored tones.

'Bye-bye.' Everyone waved as Grandpa turned the car towards the compound's exit. The guard at the gates who knew them all well gave a half wave - half salute and the big gates swung open. Ian and Valerie stood waving until the children were out of sight.

13~

Julia had packed only what mattered to her. She had included very few clothes and hardly any of her chipped crockery or grimy bed linen. The man had said on the phone that she would be provided for until the baby was born and then she would receive a lump sum and a portfolio of investments sufficient to ensure that she would never, for the rest of her life, have to live in squalid surroundings, scrimp, save, beg or borrow again. That was, of course, when she handed the baby over. Until then she would be looked after by his employers. He didn't name them and she didn't ask. She was too much in awe of him to dare to ask for credentials. He seemed to expect her to recognise that such arrangements were made for the fortunate few and that she should not presume to question.

There were conditions, of course. She was to cut all ties with her former friends and family. Well, she had no family living and her friends were mostly stoned out of their minds or waiting in doctors' waiting rooms for prescriptions that would enable them to get stoned. Julia had come to hate that way of life and had for some years looked with envy at the smart, clean, fashionable young people who came from the compounds. Now she would be one of them. Surely that was better than struggling to bring up a disabled child with no cash and nowhere of her own to live. Now she would have a house of her own and money to spend. Only the child would be missing. But then, she was young, she could have another baby and perhaps she would get married first to one of the smart young men in the compound. Would those people accept her? When her benefactor had phoned he had implied that she must no longer dress like an Outsider if she wanted to be accepted. He had seemed to be saying that he would take her shopping. Shopping! That was for Insiders. Outsiders queued at give-away stations for second hand clothes, for food, for all the things they needed just to live. Everything was available free if you knew where to go for it, and the monthly government allowance, which was meant to make them all equal, made most of them lazy and careless. Sitting on her battered suitcase and watching Patches and another boy sharing a spliff, she realised that they were unlikely to notice her departure. She waited for the man to arrive, knowing with a strange aching sensation that she would no longer be part of this squalor, and wondering if there was anyone or any part of it that she would miss when it was lost to her.

His car drew up beside the broken kerb-stones. It was so silent that she was unaware of his arrival until she heard the soft clunk of the closing door and his footsteps on the pathway.

'All ready?' he said.

'Yes, as ready as I'll ever be.' She stood up.

'Just the one bag?'

'Yep.'

She thought he carried it in such a way as to avoid letting it touch his coat. I've got to cut out the persecution complex, she thought. I'll never survive if I believe everyone from now on is going to look down on me, wishing they could hold their noses.

'Said your goodbyes, have you?'

'Precious few of those.' She looked across at Patches who lifted one hand in a feeble farewell.

'Be happy,' said the other boy.

'They don't care about me,' said Julia quietly.

'That's good. We don't want you pining for your old life.'

They got into the car. Its leather interior was soft and smelt wonderful. She sat beside him in the front. Her bag was on the back seat. The battery purred into life and the car slid away, reached the main expressway and she felt it gathering speed until it seemed as if it might take off and fly.

'Lovely car,' she said.

'Rather big for you. We thought of getting you a wine-red Sedan. It'll be part of the deal - after you've had your baby.'

'What?'

'Well, you'll need to get about. It's not safe to walk around outside the compounds. Not all the Outsiders are as docile as those you've been living with.'

'What will they think of me - the Insiders?'

'It doesn't matter what they think. You'll be your own person. You won't have to please anyone. We'll go shopping before we get there and no one will ever know you haven't come from a perfectly respectable compound elsewhere.'

They pulled off the road into the enormous car-park of a multi-complex shopping centre. On the way up the escalator Julia watched the wall panels advertising the latest fashions identified by the names of top designers. She held her shabby jacket round her, wanting to hide the dirty, torn gear underneath.

'We'll soon have you smartened up,' said the man.

'I won't know what to choose,' said Julia.

'Don't worry,' he said, 'it's all taken care of.'

They went into a clothes department, which was conspicuously spacious and the woman in charge greeted them warmly and said that she had looked out some items for Julia to try on. In a fitting room that was bigger than her recent bedroom and furnished like a room in an embassy or grand hotel from a film, with velvet covered armchairs, some little gold stools and a three panelled mirror, she found an array of dresses and suits, skirts, trousers, blouses and outdoor clothes. There was also an assortment of underwear, nightwear and evening clothes, some very like the examples she had seen on the walls as they came up the escalator. Feeling suddenly faint she sat down on one of the chairs and held her coat even more tightly round her.

'We'll leave you to try on what you fancy. Have fun!' said the woman. She and the man departed and closed the door softly. Their discretion did nothing to help Julia and it was quite a long time before she could bring herself to undress and try on any of the clothes. Everything she tried fitted her. Some were loose and floating. Ideal for her developing pregnancy. Every garment made her unkempt hair and grimy skin look more terrible. She chose a pair of beautifully fitting trousers and a white silk blouse and put on her old coat over them. She ventured out of the room and saw the man and the woman talking at a little distance. She coughed and they looked round.

'Oh, my dear!' said the woman. 'The pants and the blouse are a perfect choice but you really will have to replace the coat too.'

She swept Julia back into the fitting room, took a black designer coat from the rail and helped her into it in exchange for her own. The man was in the doorway. 'Will that do?' the woman asked him.

'Perfectly,' he said, 'and now please pack up all the rest and we'll take them with us. My car is just outside.'

As they continued their journey the shabby holdall on the back seat was swamped with bags and boxes bearing the names of well-known and lesser-known fashion houses.

'I'm going to need some shampoo,' said Julia, ashamed at being unable to live up to the wonderful cleanliness that seemed suddenly to threaten her.

'You'll find all that sort of thing ready and waiting in your new bathroom,' he said.

They were coming into Finchley now. At Swiss Gate he pulled the car over and they stopped at the entry to the compound. Beyond the gates were grass and trees and well-spaced houses. An armed man came out of the gatehouse. He saluted the driver, calling him 'Sir'. They seemed to be expected. The guard handed over an information pack and an identification tag for Julia.

'This will open the gate automatically if you wear it,' her companion explained. 'You'll need to process it so that it incorporates your DNA. The instructions are in the pack. That ensures that no one else carrying it or wearing it will be able to get inside the compound. You're an Insider now, Julia.'

The gates swung open and they drove past some imposing houses and then turned right along the edge of a park. There were trees and beautiful stretches of grass for children.

'This is not the only park,' he said. 'This compound incorporates the old Hampstead Heath. If you take a walk up the hill, you'll find Hampstead Village and the Heath beyond. It's one of the most sought after compounds in the whole London living complex.'

'What will I do here?' Julia said. 'This lifestyle is beyond me.'

'You'll soon get used to it.'

They slowed down and came to a stop outside a small house with a red brick facade and gleaming window frames with white shutters. There was ivy growing on the wall and the front door was dark green and newly painted with a gleaming knocker of brass. It was a story-book house. The sort of house where people would have scones and jam for tea on a white tablecloth.

'This is it,' said the man. 'I'll let you go in and get used to it by yourself. I'll put your parcels on the porch and just slip away. Here are the keys. You'll find the solar central heating works well. The local midwife will call on you in a few days' time, so will a hairdresser and a voice coach, just to help you fit in with the people around here more easily. The address of your doctor and dentist are in the address book in the hallway with all the other information you might need. I hope you'll be very happy here.'

On the verge of tears, Julia got out of the car and stood rather stupidly on the porch while the man made two journeys from the car with her bag and all the new clothes. Then he got back in the car, looked at her and said,

'Go on!' and made a gesture of unlocking the door. Julia faced the house and then, as she heard him start the engine, turned and said,

'When will I see you again?'

'You may not see me,' he said. 'You'll probably see Ian, our treasurer. He'll sort out all the finances for you when the baby has arrived. Until then all your basic living expenses will be paid. You'll find a bank account with a modest sum in it and a credit card with the papers in the hall. You'll find we give you a small monthly allowance in addition to your government payment until the baby arrives. Be careful, don't spend it all at once. We want you to learn to be careful with money ready for the time when you have plenty of your own.'

'I . . . don't know what to say.'

'Be happy,' he said, echoing the boy at the commune, and quickly put the car in gear and glided away. Standing watching him go she became aware of children playing in the small park and beyond them, on the other side of the park, a number of beautiful houses, detached and standing among trees. She was holding the keys of her own house so tightly that they were digging into her hand. She turned to the door again and put the key into the lock. I didn't thank him, she thought. The door swung open easily and, after a moment, she stepped inside. The hall smelt of furniture polish and new carpets.

14~

The compounds and the Outsider districts in London, as in all big cities, were very strictly separated. So were the inhabitants of these districts. Insiders hardly ever walked about outside their compounds and almost never used public transport. They were not afraid of meeting Outsiders, there simply was no reason for it to happen. Insiders were house-proud and tended their gardens with care. It was well known that Outsiders took little care of property and would litter any area where they lived with trash. Insiders preferred a clean and hygienic environment. Outsiders owned nothing and took what they could get, discarding what they did not want as they went. They had such drugs as they needed on request, so they had no reason to rob or mug the rich to support a costly habit. Drug Barons were historic figures like pirates and highwaymen. Alcohol was expensive and was simply not on sale to Outsiders. This meant that drunkenness and violence were not part of the Outsider lifestyle. Insiders drank when it pleased them, but driving when under the influence of alcohol was a criminal offence and no Insiders would risk the loss of the Insider status for themselves and their families that would follow a conviction. City life had settled into a pattern in which Insiders and Outsiders simply did not meet, and that was how both factions liked it.

In the provinces, in small towns and villages, the division was often less marked. Some towns were very strict but in others the Outsiders were not banned from the town centre shopping zones and in some cases Outsiders worked for Insiders when the arrangement suited both. In some small villages, compounds hardly existed and Insiders and Outsiders lived in harmony, sharing the same facilities and helping each other in ways that would have been unthinkable in the big cities.

The police were a constant presence in all communities. They were a reliable and friendly body, well trained in psychology and pastoral care. They managed Insiders and Outsiders with equal tact and were trusted. Naturally, the network of compound guards was of immense help to them. Serious crime was minimal and prisons were not over-crowded.

Religious observance was an intensely private matter. The acknowledgement by all of the existence of a spiritual dimension did not lead to demonstrations or rivalries between faiths. All beliefs were valued, all were seen to have stemmed from the same spiritual awareness at the core of existence and the same aspirations arising from this. An individual's belief was his or her own business. Faith was a matter between the individual and the Deity, or universal spiritual intelligence, or the higher self, or whatever consciousness of another dimension was perceived to exist. Belief was not compulsory but, given the freedom to believe in something or nothing beyond the life of matter, most people opted for something. The most intelligent, scientific and creative minds that had graced the planet over the centuries, including Hermes Trismegistus, Jesus the Christ, Mohammed the Prophet, Gautama the Buddha, Isaac Newton, William Blake, Einstein and Carl Gustav Jung, had declared themselves aware of a spiritual dimension. In some cases, their followers had made their teaching a stick with which to beat both believers and non-believers, but that was all over now. Faith was not proclaimed publicly nor was it acceptable for one person or group to maintain or suggest that their faith was better than any other, any more than they would have suggested that one race or colour of skin was better than another. No person or group was permitted to impose his faith on others by means of evangelism or coercion. Religious observance, where it occurred, was private. Spiritual teaching covered all faiths and teachers were trained to show no kind of bias for or against a faith, nor would they have wished to do so. The philosophy of the spirit and the evidence of the spiritual dimension in life was valued and respected without being fixed to a set of beliefs or rituals. Philosophers, psychologists and spiritual advisors, such as Una, were closely related in their work and were valued and recognised by Insiders and Outsiders alike. The large religious gatherings of history had died out and smaller gatherings of like-minded people had gradually taken their place. Churches, cathedrals, synagogues and mosques were seen as precious spiritual monuments to be visited by all. Information about the beliefs and practices that had brought them into existence was available to every visitor. Compulsory prayer or attendance at ritual events were archaic practices that had become non-existent. It was no longer thought that any doctrine would save the world. Responsibility for that was seen to rest squarely on the shoulders of human beings who were recognised as struggling to come to maturity.

Piers had written extensively about society and the balance of need and fulfilment in various social groups. The present division between Insiders and Outsiders was a crude development relating to a utopian idea of his own. He believed that all people must be happier if they were able to live as they wished, having their needs met to the degree that they would be free to contribute to society with the best that was in them. This was all that he had ever wanted for himself. He believed that all human beings were innately good and that it was only the thwarting of endeavour or fulfilment that caused men and women to experience resentment, hatred or the desire to fight others or to harm them. To some degree he had been proved right. People of all nations were now free to choose their own lifestyle. If they desired to work, to be creative or inventive, or to give a service, their contribution was nurtured. If they sought the support of society without having to contribute, in old age, in illness or as a result of lassitude, they would be entitled to an appropriate income and such treatment and services as their condition demanded. Poverty and starvation were unknown. But Piers had not foreseen that idleness and even squalor were options that vast numbers of young urban dwellers would accept and even choose. The Outsiders could have cleaned up their living areas, maintained their homes, made gardens, but they did not. They were not resentful, they were not criminals, they were simply not ambitious. Piers, with his deep response to and love of philosophy and his high-minded belief in all mankind, simply could not understand it. He was not happy with the situation of divided living in the cities but he was proud of three developments that his administration had consolidated: the limits on alcohol that had eliminated violence from the Outsider communes; the provision of pure drugs to those who needed them, which had cut the need for most Outsider crime; and the final prevention of religious hatred by means of the now internationally accepted philosophy of privacy and tolerance. Each of these developments had undoubtedly grown over several generations of the World Parliament, but his own writings and his personal policies had helped to establish them with absolute security.

15~

'The great alchemical secrets were almost certainly discovered by men that we would think of as primitive. They became refined with the rise of the great civilisations of Egypt (with Hermes Trismegistus) Mesopotamia, Babylon, and among the Aztecs and the Incas. Undoubtedly Greece and Rome will have made their contribution to that refinement.' The master surveyed his class of boys, some of whom who might one day prove to be Oxbridge candidates. Several of them were doodling or gazing out of the window, one was asleep, but one was leaning forward with rapt attention. A speaker, teacher or performer needs only one affirming presence of this kind to feel that their efforts are worthwhile. The master continued. 'There is little record in Britain that alchemical studies were in any way extensive or taken seriously until the Renaissance. Dorn and Paracelsus date from this period, as does the famous Doctor John Dee in England. Pico Della Mirandola of course was an outstanding Renaissance philosopher but he was Italian. In England we cannot imagine that the philosophers and the metaphysical poets sprang up ready made from the soil of the Renaissance. There must have been a great deal of earlier work in this country. It is simply not as well documented as that of Italy and other European and Eastern countries. The British have always been lazy. They have also always been secretive. The perfidious Albion was not merely a figment of Le Marquis de Ximenez's imagination. The concept has its foundation in a national characteristic of which we have reason to feel ashamed. And we have probably paid for it many times in the loss of valuable information and historical fact that might have enriched future generations. Philosophers and alchemists of Elizabeth the First's time were eager to discuss how many angels might be able to stand on the head of a pin, or what hermetic relationship between chemicals might produce gold, but they did not let us into the secrets of their real experiments in spirituality and metaphysics. There are still people who mistakenly believe that turning lead into gold was their actual aim. That, of course, is nonsense. What they were doing was transforming gross man by means of the soul. They recognised its ability to pervade the selfish, carnal life of a human being and change it for the better. The 'Hermetic Relationship' of chemicals in a crucible, sealed in and heated together so that they merge and change each other, or explode in the attempt, was a metaphor for those human relationships in which people are held together by some compulsion and are equally caused to change. Examples of this would be the pupil/teacher relationship, the intense and meaningful friendship and, of course, marriage. We change each other. I teach you and in the process I change you. In return I am open to your responses and they are capable of changing me. Teaching is not a one-way street. People who commit themselves to anything for any length of time will be changed by it. Constant exposure to a single doctrine, good or evil, has power to change the mind in radical ways. Any study or influence can do this, philosophy, politics, religion. That is why religions have been so dangerous in the past. Are there any questions? Would anyone like to dispute what I've been saying?' The attentive boy in the second row put up his hand.

'Yes, Diamond?'

'Can any friendship be a Hermetic Relationship, sir?'

'I said so, didn't I?'

'What about enmity?'

'A profound point, well done, Diamond! Yes, we can be as fixated about our enemies as we are about our friends, often more so indeed. Either relationship, positive or negative, can bring about hermetic change.'

'How does it happen?'

'I think it depends upon the will of the participants, and yet . . . there is also an element of being trapped - or perhaps 'held' is a better word - in a hermetic relationship.'

'Have you experienced it, sir?'

'Well, I am a teacher and also a married man, Diamond, but I don't think this is the right moment for me to discuss my personal experiences in either respect. The bell will go in a matter of seconds.'

'I'm very sorry sir, I didn't mean to . . .'

The bleeper above the door began to emit a repetitive signal. The lesson was over. The boys rose in a body, some of them yawning, and took up their philosophy notebooks and moved towards the door. A school lunch, albeit uninspiring, was better than the lecture they had just endured. The master looked down at his desk. It was not worth fighting against the tide once it was on the move. However lacking in respect or courtesy their departure might be, the class had at least listened quietly. The fact that it was now making its escape without waiting for permission was a cross that had to be born. Well, there had to be some give and take. Piers approached the desk.

'Could I talk to you about this some time, sir? It's the most interesting lesson we ever have and it's always over just as it's getting really exciting.'

'Creep!' said Hugo Finch, passing unnecessarily close behind Piers in order to pinch him viciously in the back of the arm.

'That will do, Finch,' the master said. He smiled at Piers, 'A bit of hermetic enmity on offer there, Diamond, if you let yourself get drawn into it.

'I won't,' said Piers.

16~

Prune was Eden's perfect choice for an undercover agent. No one could possibly have suspected her and people who got to know her soon felt able to talk unguardedly in her presence, believing that her vacant expression meant that she was not listening. This was a huge advantage and an additional advantage was Prune's phenomenal memory. She could repeat conversations word for word with remarkable accuracy, even when she had understood less than half of what was said. But, there was one major drawback. Prune was a chatterbox. She was often shy and monosyllabic at a first meeting with people, but as soon as she felt at home with them she would spill out everything that came into her head without reserve. This often included the most recent instructions that Eden had given her or his opinions on matters that were way above her head. 'Eden says,' was her favourite introduction to any topic. She was quite capable, for instance, of informing Una of everything that Eden thought about Piers' most recent actions on the world stage and she would finish by saying, 'and he told me not to repeat this to anybody.' With Una, of course, any information was safe, but Eden knew, and Una had reinforced the knowledge many times, that Prune could not be trusted to be discreet. She had to be told as little as possible about anything that mattered, and any project in which Eden had to use her, worked best if it could be presented to her as a kind of game. There were two responses that Prune really enjoyed from her listeners, laughter and shock. Eden was becoming more and more canny at using these triggers when he employed her to gain information.

Prune enjoyed living rough. It meant wearing their oldest and warmest clothes, going for days without having to have a shower or a bath, eating chips out of plastic bags and finding places to sleep outdoors where the police wouldn't move them on. When Eden was on the prowl they often went close to one of the Outsider communes but never attempted to stay there overnight.

'We don't want to catch something,' Eden always said. Prune didn't know what sort of thing they might catch but she was sure he was right.

This time they approached a seedy looking commune and stopped on the edge where a broken down children's playground offered a chance of sitting down and eating the take-out meal Eden had bought for them at a battery station. The food was cheap and synthetic, the sort Prune loved and Una was horrified by. Eden finished eating and sat watching the entrance of a drug provision centre about a hundred yards away.

'Are we looking for someone?' Prune asked.

'Shut up!' said Eden.

'Lovely,' said Prune.

'What do you mean, lovely?'

'Your manners.'

'You can't talk. At least I didn't lick my carton. You're not exactly ladylike, are you?' Prune stopped licking the gravy out of the corners of her carton and threw it on the ground. 'Pick that up,' said Eden.

'Why? This place is a dump. Look at all the rubbish lying around.'

'We're not here to make it worse.'

'Where's your carton, then?'

'I've put it in my backpack. I shall throw it in a trash pit when we pass one. Give me yours. Pick it up, Prune.' She did as she was told reluctantly.

'I don't want to go near one of those trash pits. They stink.'

'Of course they do until they're filled in. There are plenty of them, though. They don't have to leave any of them open for long. It's when people chuck stuff away and it festers for days in the street before it's collected that you get a lot of smelly rotting stuff collected together on the top.'

'Why can't they grind everything up like we do? It's easier to bury then. Or it goes down the drain.'

'Most Outsiders don't have access to a grinder.'

'We're lucky then.'

'Yes, we're lucky.'

'Where are we going to sleep tonight?'

'We'll find somewhere nice, you wait and see.

'Not by one of those pits?'

'No.'

'We could sleep here. I'd like that. I could get to know one of those children over there - and tell them how mean you are to me when you're on one of your secret missions!'

'You certainly could not. When we're on a secret mission, Prune, you don't tell anyone about it. If you start talking about our walkabout adventures, I'll never take you on one again.'

'That's not fair.'

'Prune,' he pulled her round to stand in front of him, 'listen to me very carefully. You must not talk to people about me or about anything I do unless I tell you to. This is our secret life and it's very important that no one knows about it. If ever anyone asks you where we've been when we're out on the road like this, you must say you can't remember.'

'I always remember everything.'

'I know you do, but you have to say you've forgotten these times. Do you understand me?'

'I suppose so.' Prune was wriggling in his grasp.

'Prune, look at me, have you heard and understood me properly?'

'Yes.'

'I mean this, Prune. Our lives could be at risk at some time in the future if you talk about what happens on these journeys.'

'Our lives!'

'Yes!'

'We might be killed stone dead, you mean?'

'Yes, that is exactly what I mean.'

'And I can't tell Una?'

'No. I'll tell Una if I want her to know. It might put her in danger too. We are only safe and our friends are only safe if you keep everything completely secret between us.'

'Why can't I talk to Una?' Prune was grizzling and refusing to look at him.

'I said completely secret between us. Us. You and me. Got it.'

'Yes.'

A young man in a distinctive patched coat was coming out of the drug users' centre. Eden let go of Prune and said quickly,

'You sit here and don't move. I'll be back in a few minutes.'

'Can I come with you?'

'No.' Eden was moving away.

'Oh, Eee-den,'

'No, Prunella. Sit still and be quiet and wait for me, right?'

'Right.' Resigned to her boring fate Prune settled herself on the middle of the sea-saw and tried unsuccessfully to work its dirty, heavy plank up and down on either side of her.

The young man was coughing badly. Eden came up to him as he was taking a half smoked joint out of his pocket.

'That won't do you much good.' Eden said kindly.

'That's my business,' said the boy. He couldn't have been more than about twenty but his face was haggard.

'I'm looking for a young woman who used to live in this commune,' said Eden.

'Oh, yes?' The young man was not much interested.

'I think you might be able to help me. I believe you know her quite well.'

'You been spying on us?'

'Not at all. I simply know about you because a friend of mine, who this girl approached for help, was able to describe you as someone who was good to her.'

'I'm not good to people, much.'

'Then I expect you know who I mean. I'm hoping you can tell me where she's gone.'

'Gone, has she?'

'Yes, gone from here. Do you know where she went?'

'How should I know? People come and go.'

'I believe she was pregnant.'

The young man looked at Eden for a long time before saying,

'It wasn't mine, if that's what you're after.'

'That's not what I'm asking.'

'A man in a flash car took her away.'

'Did you see him?'

'Yea, sort of.'

'Could you describe him?'

'Rich looking. He had a hat on and a coat like - cashmere, I should think it was. He had leather gloves. He gave her his handkerchief. She gave it to me before she left. It's here, look. 'He took from his pocket a screwed up grey ball of a handkerchief but it was finest linen and had a finely embroidered monogram, 'ES' in one corner. Eden looked at the monogram and returned the handkerchief to the boy.

'Thank you,' he said, 'that's very helpful.'

'I dunno where she is,' said the boy. 'Perhaps she's living with him. Perhaps he loves her. Perhaps he's living off her immoral earnings. Either way, good luck to her, I say.'

'What's her name?'

'Are you a policeman?'

'Do I look like a policeman?'

'No, but you talk like one.'

52

'I'm travelling with my sister. We're looking for a place to stay.'

'Well, I can't help you. Our place is crammed full.'

'I wasn't asking you that. I just want to know what the girl's name is. The friend I mentioned thinks she may need help and I'd like to be able to locate her and reassure my friend that she's all right.'

'I'd like to know she's alright. If I tell you her name will you come back and tell me how she is - if you find her?'

'Yes, I'll do that.'

'Where's your sister?'

'Over there.' Prune was now lying on her tummy on the see-saw and lifting her arms up and down from time to time in an imitation of some sort of bird.

'She's one of those mongol children, isn't she?'

'She has Down's Syndrome.'

'Poor little kid.'

'She's happy enough.'

'Julia's baby was going to be like that.'

'What?'

'I said Julia's baby was going to be one of those Down's babies. I expect the man will have got her to have an abortion. That's what they do now, isn't it?'

'Yes,' said Eden. 'I believe it is.'

'I'd really like to know how she is,' said the boy. 'Julia Barton, that's her name.'

'Thank you,' said Eden, 'I'm really very grateful to you.'

'No sweat,' said the boy and shuffled off towards the commune trying to light his joint as he went.

17~

'What would you like to do today?' said the children's grandmother. She was collecting up the breakfast plates and observing that they were satisfyingly clean, despite insistence from Benjamin that he hated tomato corncake. It was the last day of the children's visit and their grandmother wanted to give them a treat before they went home to their heavily controlled, professional-executive compound in London. Lucy looked at her grandmother thoughtfully, considering the options.

'What do you suggest?'

'Well, there's the gardens across the way. We could have a picnic outside. Or we could walk a little way and take our picnic to the fields on the edge of the compound where we can see the downs. I know you like the downs.'

'Could we go outside the wire fence?' Benjamin was always wanting to get beyond the safety limits.

'You know where it's possible to go and where it's not.'

'But couldn't we?' Lucy's voice was almost pleading, 'Couldn't we, just for once, go outside the compound and have a picnic in the real countryside?'

'Yes,' said Benjamin, 'do let's.'

'That would be a 'real' experience.' 'Real' was the 'in' word of the moment. Young people who would once have said 'fab' or 'cool' to denote extreme approval, now underlined the unreality of their third millennium existence by calling anything unusual or pleasurable 'real'.

'Not possible,' said their grandmother, 'as you very well know.'

'Because of Outsiders,' said Lucy.

'Not only that,' her grandmother was adamant. 'I'm in charge of you. I don't want to go out of phone signal range. I'm not going to let you take the slightest risk. What would your mother say?'

'When we've been driving about here,' Lucy said archly, 'I haven't seen even one Outsider.'

'You sound disappointed,' said her grandmother.

'Well, you wouldn't see them near the express ways,' said Benjamin. 'They don't go near fast moving traffic. What would be the point? There are always too many police cars about.'

'Why would you want to look for them?' their grandmother was puzzled.

'I don't know,' said Lucy. 'They interest me. I think they're so – real!'

'You wouldn't go near one?' her grandmother said with a warning tone.

'I might,' said Lucy, leaning back in her chair. 'They're interesting. A lot more interesting than my family.'

'That's silly talk,' her grandmother said sharply.

'You'd better not let Mum hear you say that,' said Benjamin, glad for once to be able to adopt a superior attitude to his eminently superior sister.

'She won't hear unless someone tells her and makes trouble,' said Lucy in a mildly threatening tone.

'I know where I want to go,' said Benjamin, cutting across the deteriorating atmosphere.

'Oh, yes?' Lucy's bored tone was intensified for his benefit.

'Where would you like to go, Ben?' His grandmother asked kindly.

'I'd like to go to the sea.'

'Don't be silly,' said Lucy quietly.

'Might see lots of 'them',' said Benjamin.

'Real!' said Lucy. 'Let's.'

At the far end of the room their grandfather put down the book he was reading.

'Why not?' he said, 'We've got all day and it's their last day here. Let's take them to the sea.'

The whole coastline of the British Isles was dotted with hydro-electric sea-water reservoirs. Every few miles the sea had been pumped into artificial, salt-water lakes of sufficient size to create a force of water that could be dammed up and released into a gully on the landward side. These gullies varied from sixty to eighty feet in depth, and the descending water was then recycled back into the reservoir to facilitate a continuous process of power generation which was then fed into the national grid. If any reservoir level dropped more water was pumped in from the sea. If the reservoir overflowed this happened on the seaward side where there was a slight dip in the retaining wall which was designed to allow surplus water to spill out, back into the ocean.

The Insider compounds all had swimming pools. The Outsiders had no such luxury and crowded to the coast in good weather to swim in the reservoirs. Because of this the Insider population avoided going within sight of the sea except in their own coastal compounds, of which there were many, some very luxurious. Lucy and Benjamin's grandparents knew no one who lived in a coastal compound and so it was essential, if the children were to have the rare visit to the sea that they craved, that they went to an open area of the coast.

They arrived before lunchtime and, after a short walk on a deserted and rather chilly beach, went into a cafe for drinks to warm them up. It was a cheap cafe, frequented by Outsiders. The children and their grandparents looked overly clean and smart among the sparse clientele. Lucy looked round enraptured. This was the kind of adventure she had hoped for.

18~

'I wish I was part of a family like that.' Prune sat with her elbows on the cafe table gazing at the two children laughing with their grandparents.

'They're enjoying themselves,' said Eden, 'but Insiders have no heart.'

She looked at the group across the cafe and wondered if he meant this literally or whether it was one of the things clever people say when they really mean something else.

'No heart at all?'

'None at all, Prune, none at all. Not one of them.'

'How do they stay alive, then?'

'By means of their money and their wits.'

Prunella watched his face carefully. Wit was something he was rich in. Everyone said so. 'A witty man, your brother,' they'd say. And Prunella would feel proud of him because the comment was always forthcoming when he had just said something impressive to make someone laugh although, often, she had neither understood the words nor been able to see the joke herself. But she didn't mind about that. She was used to it.

Prunella was much younger than Eden and her other illustrious brother, Piers. After Prunella was born and her mother had died of the Cranes-Patterson virus, an un-treatable infection that attacked women after childbirth and was almost always fatal, Prune had grown up in the care of her father and had hardly known her brother and her half-brother. In her experience they had always been grown men, whilst she still thought of herself as a child. Now that she was nearly twenty she imagined that she would soon have to start thinking of herself as grown up too. After all, she was much older now than Eden had been when she was a tiny new baby. And yet the idea of herself as an adult seemed improbable. Piers had been an adult when she was a toddler and Eden had seemed like one too. He had been at school and Piers, in his twenties, had already been at Oxford.

Prunella was not stupid and she knew that she was different from most other people. Her father who had brought her up had carefully explained that Down's Syndrome children did not grow up to be quite like ordinary people. She had listened to this but it had taken time for her to understand the extent of it. She couldn't remember when she had first recognised that she was different. The knowledge had crept up on her gradually, partly as a result of the fact that people had often been at such pains to be kind and to say nice, careful, reassuring things to her for no reason that she could understand, and partly because she had become gradually aware that her family all made allowances for her in a way that other families did not need to do with their younger members. Eden was the only person who had never been careful like that. He had always treated her as rudely as he treated anyone else and for this she loved him best in all the world. She would have done anything for Eden.

'Insider kids!' He said. 'Too clever for their own good. They don't know they're born!'

This too was puzzling for Prunella, but that was nothing unusual. She had a completely literal mind, a fact that her brother had never understood, and it put quite a lot of his conversation beyond the reach of her comprehension. No one had ever explained to her the niceties of metaphor, sarcasm or even simple irony. Prunella's world was a wonderland of inexplicable strangeness in which everyone spoke from time to time in coded messages which they understood but she could not. This never worried or saddened her. She simply accepted it as the natural order of things and went on her way with a sense of wonder that is lost to most people by the age of seven.

'Who are they, then?'

'A couple of rich kids with their grandparents, obviously,' he said, as if the word 'rich' were a dire insult. 'Eaters of the lotus.'

This comment too was way beyond Prunella so she ignored it and simply sat and watched the group. The girl had long blond hair, shining with health from probable frequent washings with expensive shampoos. She laughed mockingly at the jokes made by the boy. His jokes were comprehensible to Prune. She liked the look and sound of him but she would have liked to be the girl.

'Stop gawping at them.' Eden said. 'You don't want to draw attention to us.' She decided to try a laugh like the girl had done, baring her teeth she leaned back and then looked at him very seriously with her chin tucked well down, giving a scornful cackle.

'For God's sake be quiet,' he said. 'What's the matter with you? You're not feeling ill, are you?'

'No!' She shifted sulkily in her chair. She didn't like being misunderstood. She had wanted him to say she was just like the girl over there. For a moment she had felt as if she was that girl. But it had only been for a moment.

'Look at the boy,' he said, indicating briefly with a lift of one finger, his hand hung limp from his forearm which rested on the back of his chair. Prunella looked.

'Do you mean the one telling the jokes?'

'That's the one.'

'What about him?'

'See if you can strike up a conversation with him when they get up to go. He's about your size.'

'I don't know what to do,' said Prune sulkily.

'Just strike up a conversation with him - briefly - casually.'

'Shall I ask him where he lives?'

'Of course not, idiot! I know where he lives. That's the last thing you want to ask him.'

'What then?'

'Ask him if he knows Julia Barton.'

'Who's she?'

'No one, dear child. I don't suppose such a person exists but that's not the point. You want to ask him something you can refer to again when you see him again, get it?'

'No, 'cos I'm not going to be seeing him again, am I?' She bit her lip and shook her head. Eden knew this was a bad sign. 'You might be seeing him quite often in the future if you get this right today. Don't you want to do it?'

'Yes, but I don't see.'

'Alright, my darling.' He was speaking now with infinite patience. 'Wait till they all get up to leave and then you get up too and go towards the 'ladies' room' and on your way say to him, "Hello, are you a friend of Julia's?"

'He'll think I'm stupid asking that.'

'No he won't. Now, Prunella, listen to me. You say that and then if he says "Yes" you say, "Do you know her well? She's a friend of my brother's".'

'Julia Barton?'

'Yes.'

'Is she a friend of yours?'

'Yes, in a way.'

'Supposing he says he doesn't know her?'

59

'Then you leave it and come back to me.'

'What's he going to think?'

'He won't think anything. He'll probably think you're sweet.'

'Sweet? Me? He won't think that. He'll think I'm stupid and ugly compared to his sister.'

'Oh, little Prune,' he said. 'You really are a wow sometimes. You never cease to amaze me.'

She didn't know whether to be pleased or disappointed at this and while she was considering the matter, the group at the table began to get up and suddenly she felt herself propelled by Eden's unrelenting hand in the direction of the boy.

She stumbled slightly across the carpet in the vague direction of the door to the ladies' room and nearly bumped into him. He saw her instantly and put out a hand to steady her.

'Woops!' He said in a kind, friendly voice. 'Don't go falling over.'

She smiled at him, slightly breathless from nervousness at the importance of her mission.

'Sorry,' she said. She glanced back at Eden but he was sitting with his back to her and his face half hidden by his hand. 'Are you a friend of Julia's?' she asked, a little too loudly, hoping Eden would hear and be pleased with her.

'Julia who?' said the boy.

'Julia Mm . . Barton.' She had got it right; she knew she had.

'No,' said the boy, 'We don't know any Julia Barton, do we Lucy?'

'No,' said Lucy, 'We don't live round here. We live in London.'

'So do we,' said Prune, 'Do you eat lotuses?'

'What?' The boy's voice was surprised. He laughed.

'Prunella!' Eden's voice was anything but warm, 'Stop bothering those people.'

'But I'm only . . .'

'It's all right,' said the grandfather. 'She's no bother at all. She's a sweet little soul.'

'Come on, Ben,' said the girl with long hair. She paused to look back at Eden from the door.

'So you don't know a Julia?' said Prunella, valiantly trying to complete her assignment.

'No,' said the boy, still speaking in a kind and interested way. 'I don't think so.' Lucy began moving slowly in the direction of Eden.

'Come on!' said the grandmother. 'We're going now. Bye bye.'

'Bye bye,' said Prune, 'See you in London maybe.'

'Leave it,' snapped Eden between clenched teeth.

'That might be 'real!' said Lucy.

'I have to go now,' Prunella said politely.

'Me too,' said Lucy, looking at Eden with regret. She turned and ran towards the door where her exit was engulfed in a tirade of whispered remonstrances. Prunella went back to the table and sat down.

'She didn't like me,' she said.

'Who?'

'She didn't like me. She only liked you.'

He looked at her fondly. 'What nonsense you do talk.'

'I don't,' she said with determination, 'I don't at all. But you were right about one thing. The old man thought I was sweet. He said so.'

19~

'How do you heat this place in the winter?'

'Solar power.' Una bent down to take a pot of stew out of the oven.

'Where are the panels? Do you want any help with that?' The scientist Robin Sheldon watched her bringing the heavy pot to the table.

'No thanks, I'm fine. The panels are on the roof above the bathroom and guest bedrooms. That wing of the house faces south and I keep the trees cut back on that side to allow plenty of sun through.'

'What capacity tank do you heat?'

'I've no idea, but it's a large one. There's always plenty of hot water and the house is warm enough for me. I don't like sweltering heat, anyway. It makes you sleepy. I hate to feel sleepy in the day time.'

'Your self-sufficiency does you great credit,' he said.

'I wouldn't want it any other way. Nor would you.'

'Up to fifty years ago, when we were children, there were a good many people living like this. Now I honestly believe that your place here and my farm are the only ones left.'

'Your place is much bigger than this. You have quite a team helping you to run it. I couldn't afford that.'

'Nor could I if I hadn't inherited the land and the money to run it.' He reached out eagerly as Una handed him a plate of stew and ate hungrily. 'Wonderful! I haven't tasted food like this since I left home a week ago.'

Una sat down opposite to him saying,

'Do you rely on solar power at home?'

'No. One of our buildings used to be a water mill. We harness the leet water that used to power that and it powers our own generator. We make more electricity than we can use. We sell it on to the national grid. It's quite lucrative.'

'That's even better than self-sufficiency, making a profit from the state.'

'But, Una, do you realise the obscene degree of dependency of most of the population?'

'Of course, why do you think I live out here like this?'

'Most of the compounds have some solar heating of course but they take the bulk of their power from the national grid and that means the nation has a continuing dependency on nuclear power stations. Unlike you they do want sweltering heat. Do you know, most Insiders in Britain demand a warmer atmosphere in their house during the winter than they expect on a normal summer's day.'

'I can well believe it.'

'The cost of maintaining the compounds runs into billions.'

'The Insiders seem to be able to afford it.'

'I wish Piers would look at the possibility of committing to solar energy on a world scale.'

'That would cost, surely.'

'At the outset, yes, but once it was up and running the saving would be huge.'

'You sound as if you've thought a lot about it. Is this the latest of your projects?'

'I'll show you when we've finished eating. I've got all the paperwork and plans with me. I've been touting them round London, trying to get a minister or a member of the cabinet or a fellow scientist or even a press baron to take an interest.'

'And?'

'Nothing. Most of them were 'too busy' to see me. Those who did find the time soon remembered an important appointment that was pending and made their escape.'

'But why? I haven't seen the plans yet, but I know from your past work and from the success of your own life style that what you envisage works out in practice. You've got a Nobel Prize, for heaven's sake!'

'That was a long time ago, before everything settled down to this highly lucrative arrangement in which society has trapped itself. Too many people are making money, and too many people are living comfortably as a result, for anyone to want to rock the boat.'

'But the scientists…? They must want to see power production made safer for the sake of the future of the planet. Nuclear power is efficient but it's not safe in the long term and renewing the power plants and removing the waste is increasingly dangerous, it must be.'

'It is. But scientists are a strange bunch. They maintain their own status quo by closing ranks against maverick innovations. Those at the top decide precisely who is allowed to make a break-through. Peer-review is far more important than genuine progress or true inspiration. To have my ideas accepted I would have to give up my rural way of life and go and live in one of the top London compounds. I would have to socialise with the top brass of science, government and the press, especially the scientific press, and I would have to boot-lick and beg for approval and wait my turn to have my ideas considered. They are hugely competitive. I am an Outsider in every sense of the world. While they don't rate me as one of themselves they will never rate my work.'

'Robin, that is terrible. Is it really true?'

'It's always been true. Nowadays it's worse than ever. The whole of society depends on a financial stability that is rooted in the supremacy of a small minority of very wealthy men and women. If you're not one of them, or at least, in with them, you don't have a hope in hell of getting your ideas even considered. - Nobel Prize or no Nobel Prize.'

'But Piers is not like that.'

'Oh, Piers? No, he's way above all that. So far above that he has no notion where his advisors get their ideas from. No doubt he believes that the best are God-given, but what he doesn't know is that God may speak to others outside the circle of his carefully chosen ones.'

'Will you show me your plans?'

'Willingly.'

They cleared the table and the plans were laid out. The proposition was simple. The pylons of the British national grid which criss-crossed the country, many of which were due for replacement, should each carry a pair of solar panels. These would trap the sun's rays and convert the heat into electrical power which could be fed straight into the grid and put to use on a country wide basis. This would mean that, wherever there was sunshine, the grid was being replenished and no one would be dependent upon good weather in their own area for their heating and lighting to function at full strength.

'After initial trials in this country and a nation wide installation, the plan could be extended to include the whole of Europe,' said Robin. 'That would mean that a continental grid could serve all countries and the southern areas would up the power of the more northerly territories. Well? - what do you think of it?'

'It sounds too simple and obvious to be possible. I mean, I think it's wonderful. Surely it would bring down the cost of electrical power?'

'To about a tenth of what it costs now.'

'People must want this.'

'People who are making a fortune out of the present system won't want it.'

'But it would make nuclear power stations obsolete.'

'Quite. That's the beauty of it.'

'Why don't you send it direct to Piers? You've met him. He's sure to remember you. He'd be enormously interested. Don't bother with the British government. Go straight to the very top.'

'And if his own scientific advisors persuade him, as they will, that it's a foolhardy scheme, he'll shelve it without even discussing it with me?'

'I don't think he'd do that.'

'It's possible he too likes things the way they are?'

'I don't believe so.'

'If I throw everything away by sending all this to Geneva, I'll never have another chance. I might do better to approach the Swedes or the Icelandic government. Their climates must make the idea appealing to them, but then they'd need the whole of Europe to be involved before it would be worth their while to commit to it. Those Northern countries don't have enough sunshine to rely on solar power all the year round.'

'Robin,' Una was speaking a little hesitantly, 'would you leave a copy of these plans here for a few weeks?'

'Of course I've got several copies with me. I'd hoped to leave them with various people but they wouldn't let me.'

'Leave a copy with me, will you?'

'Here.' Robin took another envelope of plans from his case. 'That's a full set. Keep it. A present from me. Do what you like with it. - Only, don't send it to Piers Diamond or anyone else without my permission.'

20~

When they were living rough Eden and Prune carried everything they
needed in back-packs. Prune always loved it at first. It meant days
without a proper wash and they slept under the stars if the weather was
good. Sometimes Eden needed her to do a little observing for him or to
strike up an innocent conversation with someone. But eventually, when
they had been on the road for a while, Prune would become fractious.
She didn't mind her own body odour but, after a while, it was more than
Eden could stand. It was then he would deliver her to Una to get cleaned
up and to regain her equilibrium with a bit of extra home comfort and
some good nights of unbroken sleep. This was usually at a point when he
had things to do that could not be managed with the encumbrance of
Prune in tow. It was an altogether satisfactory arrangement and, since
Prune adored Una and was always happy to stay with her, Eden had the
best of all possible worlds; an accomplice that no one would suspect of
devious intentions and a baby-sitter for Prune when the need arose.

This time, after their trip to the seaside, they went to the west country.
It made a nice change from the London area. Outsiders were less
numerous in many provincial towns and they got off the train at a small
cathedral city where, unlike London, the cathedral itself was not inside a
compound or a restricted zone, but stood on neutral ground among other
beautiful historic buildings. It was a pleasure to walk freely on the
cathedral green. They ate their fish and chips there and Prune pointed
to the hefty flying buttresses of the south wall.

'Look at those little caves under the arches. We could sleep in one of
those.'

'Good idea,' said Eden.

'Would anyone mind?'

'I don't suppose anyone would look there. Most of the homeless
Outsiders try to get a bench for the night. You'd find a lot at the train
station or the bus station.'

'But we're not homeless Outsiders.'

'No.'

'So they won't mind where we go.'

'They won't know the difference between us and the homeless now we're away from our house.'

'Can't they tell?'

'Of course not. That's the whole point. When we live as homeless Outsiders, other Outsiders trust us and talk to us. We don't want them to know who we really are.'

'So can we come back and sleep here?'

'I don't see why not.'

That afternoon they took a train trip into Cornwall and Eden went to look for a woman who lived in a commune just beyond the station where they got off the train. Prune was left to her own devices by the gate of a field where a friendly pony was glad to have his face stroked and to be fed a handful of grass from time to time. Prune could remain entranced for a very long time in such circumstances and Eden's only advice was that she must avoid speaking to anyone and, if she was forced to explain her presence, only to say that she was waiting for her brother who was visiting a friend. He knew from experience that Prune would not be seen as a threat to anyone, nor did she look as if she might be worth kidnapping. Her quaintness and innocence were her protection and, provided she did not talk too much, which she was always disinclined to do with strangers, she was a perfectly safe ally.

Eden found the woman, a dark skinned, sad faced person of Afro-Caribbean descent, and learned, as he had expected, that her daughter had been set up in a house of her own in a compound near London by a wealthy organisation whose name the mother did not know. She was not allowed to visit her daughter but she believed the girl, whose name was Ebbie, had had an illegitimate child which had been hushed up. She guessed this because the last time she had seen her daughter she had been suffering from morning sickness and, when her mother had suggested that pregnancy might be the cause, Ebbie had been unreasonably angry in denying it. Later the mother had gone to the outer London commune where her daughter had lived and found that she had become pregnant and that soon after realising it she had disappeared. Later still an older woman from Ebbie's old commune had stopped off with her on the way to Penzance and had said that there was a rumour that Ebbie was now employed as a servant in a London compound and was living in a staff apartment block belonging to the company that had taken her away. But they had so many apartment blocks all over London and all of them were guarded so there was no means of knowing where Ebbie was.

Eden and Prune came back to the cathedral city at nightfall and curled up under the protective arch of one of the buttresses. No one saw them there. No one disturbed them and with their packs for pillows, and the light thermal blankets they carried for warmth giving them a double covering as they huddled close together, they had a surprisingly good night's sleep.

The next morning they took the train back to London where Eden went to a public library to search on a computer terminal for recorded information on a finance company or organisation of which he did not yet know the name. He did however know the identity of one of the managing directors. The librarian was used to Outsiders who wanted to use computers to look up new sources of medication or to find spaces in communes in other areas. She assumed that Eden was one such. Occasionally those who could afford it paid for cyber-space time and put on the helmet and spent a short, blissful period in a world they could control and in which they had no worries. This form of recreational entertainment was highly addictive and libraries sometimes had difficulty prizing down-and-outs away from the helmets, even when the screen had gone dark because their money had run out. Some communes had invested in cyber gear because it kept troublesome individuals quiet for hours on end, until it got broken. Used to the usual outsider demands the Librarian was content to let Eden, a quiet, well-spoken man despite his scruffy appearance, use a computer without her intervention, and to allow his odd little sister to play on a nearby console. She liked the pair. She would have helped them if she could, but when they were leaving and she offered help if they needed it they said they were fine and went off together looking friendly and contented in a way that made her quite envious.

21 ~

The reception at the Mansion House in the City of London was over and Piers and his entourage returned to the hotel at eleven thirty. Piers dismissed all his security men but David and one other remained on night duty. David was to take the cold job on the fire escape. The other man was to mount guard in the hotel corridor. There was a chair beside a little table fixed to the wall near the lift shaft. The stairs were beyond. David gave the man permission to sit on the chair rather than stand outside the door to Piers' suite. No one could get past him there, after all. The man was grateful for such consideration from the boss. He would have an unusually comfortable night sitting there. David knew this and winked at him before he returned to Piers.

'Get out the foot pump first,' said Piers, 'it's on the top.'

'Got it.' David placed the old-fashioned foot pump on the floor by the bed.

'Now we unfold Esmeralda.' Laughing like schoolboys the two men unrolled the inflatable doll and placed her on the bed. With the nozzle of the pump attached to her navel she was quick to swell up and was soon lying there with a coy, stupid expression, and her exaggerated tits pointing ceilingwards.

'Couldn't you have done better than that?' said David, turning her over with a flick of the hand and sending her flying off the other side of the bed.

'Careful,' said Piers. 'You don't want to puncture her. Pick her up.'

'You could say her whole purpose is to be punctured. Where does the prick go?' He peered between her legs. 'Oh, I see, vaginal or anal, front or back, you've got the choice.'

'Don't be coarse.'

'I bet you never even looked.'

'No, David, as a matter of fact I never did. I find it tragic that some people need this sort of thing. Think of the loneliness.'

'It's probably their own fault. And surely a woman, any woman, would be preferable to this.'

'In the mail order catalogue it said, "Esmeralda never says no." Don't you think that's sad? I think it's infinitely sad. It made me think of all those poor disappointed men whose wives refuse them night after night. There must be plenty of them or they wouldn't make these things.'

'Was she expensive?'

'No. She was the cheapest on the list. I didn't need refinements.'

'I wonder what the refinements might be?'

'Don't ask.'

'Kinky gear, leather straps or rubber bits I guess,'

'I don't want to know what goes on in the murkier areas of your mind, Dave, thanks. Put her down, will you?'

David was holding Esmeralda by the arm. They looked a very bizarre couple side by side by the hotel bed. David gave the doll a mock passionate kiss and deposited her on top of the quilt. 'You can French Kiss her too,' he said. 'Just think - she'd need sterilising after a day or two.'

'Shut up and put her under the covers. You're making me wish I hadn't taken you into my confidence.'

'How long have you been on this caper?'

'Quite a few years.'

'She's not young then, Esmeralda? And you really believed that I or the team would think this was you if we looked in to check on your safety during the night?'

'Well, obviously you did think so up to now.'

'Yes, well, I have to admit we don't look in that often. We do respect your privacy. Most nights we stay outside.'

'That's what I've always relied on.'

'But where do you put her during the day?'

'In the wardrobe.'

'You mean, if we needed to search your rooms - for an intruder, say - we'd open the wardrobe and she'd fall out.'

'She was usually in her bag. But not always, I must admit. In a big wardrobe she can be concealed quite well behind a few suits and winter coats.'

'So could a terrorist, Piers. I can just see the headlines. "Venezuelan chief of police discovers inflatable sex partner in First Minister's hotel room." You could be toppled by this. In some people's minds a prostitute would be preferable.'

'Surprising as it may seem, I would speak the truth and I think a lot of people would sympathise with my need to have a few hours to myself.'

'To spend the night with a woman?'

'That phrase gives a totally false impression, and you know it. I would certainly never mention her. She was my stepmother's dearest friend and the family relies on her completely. She is my only reliable link with my roots. I never know where my half-brother is and I don't want to know what he's up to. It's a family thing. It's no one's business but mine. But I wouldn't have her put in the spotlight for anything in the world. I won't have her put in danger either. My visits to her have always been secret and they're going to remain so.'

'You think the media would give up before they found out where it is you go?'

'Probably not. But this is all hypothetical, David. In future I shall take you with me and the plan will be amended as you see fit. Okay?'

'Okay.' David was examining the light fittings in some detail.

'What are you looking for?'

'I'm just hoping this room isn't bugged.'

'I never speak a name in a situation like this.'

'You've said Esmeralda's name.'

'Fair point. I've probably ruined her reputation, though I seem to remember it was you who listed her credentials. I imagined you'd checked for bugs before we arrived.'

'I'm checking now. It looks all right. The boys will have changed all the light-bulbs and done a fairly thorough check before we came in.'

'Nothing to worry about then.'

'No, but I do like to do my own check.'

'Carry on then, I'll put Esmeralda to bed.' He took the doll and placed it under the bedclothes with only the dark hair showing. It was half turned to the pillow so that the prominent breasts were not evident. 'How's that?'

'Well, I do admit,' said David grudgingly, 'that, if I looked in during the night, I would never suspect it wasn't you.'

'Exactly,' said Piers.

'Cheating your own security team with such a ridiculous device is a little galling for them, or for me, at least.'

'I understand that. I'm very sorry. It was only our friendship that made me give the game away to you.'

'And the fact that I insisted on a guard on your fire-escape after the little debacle in Cairo.'

'You've never guarded fire escapes in England.'

'And so I changed the policy. And so you had to tell me the truth.'

'Well, that's all right. I can trust you.'

'Oh, yes, you can trust me. The fact that you've been hoodwinking me for years and putting yourself in appalling danger is the problem. I'm supposed to look after you at every moment. Guarding Esmeralda is a little beneath the standard of my employment contract. Did it never occur to you what fools I and the team would have looked if there had been a crisis?'

'Well, you were still guarding me in a sense.'

'So what do we do now?'

'We put on these.' Piers produced two crumpled sports suits with hooded tops and two pairs of running shoes. 'We go jogging. I think these are your size.'

'Me! Jogging!'

'You're fit, aren't you? It won't hurt you to be fitter.' David pulled on the shoes. They fitted comfortably.

'And exactly where does this woman live? Where are we going?'

'Wait and see.'

The two men, dressed alike and with their hoods up, descended the fire escape and left the hotel grounds unseen a little after midnight. They jogged the short distance to Paddington station. David, as instructed, purchased two tickets for Reading and Piers went into a public phone box. He dialled Una's number and when she answered said,

'I'm arriving with David on the half-past midnight train from Paddington.'

'I'll meet you.'

'Thanks.'

The train was quite full but not crowded. Piers and David shared a table with a middle-aged man who looked the type who would have been a farmer in earlier days. Trains were for Outsiders. Rail travel cost next to nothing. The dirty, run-down service was maintained by the government for the poor. Safety was a priority but wear and tear were so much part of Outsider life that the carriages were allowed to deteriorate quite badly before they were replaced. Some of the passengers were getting high on a shared joint at a table a little distance away. Several elderly people were dozing. A mother with two children was having trouble persuading the youngest, who was about four years old, to settle down and stop grizzling. Not one of them recognised the man in the crumpled grey tracksuit and trainers sitting silently among them with his friend. Piers kept his hood up throughout the journey. On the front of an evening paper that someone had left behind Piers saw a picture of himself, with David in the background, arriving at the reception.

'Put your hood on,' David flipped the hood up quickly and folded his arms, slumping down in the uncomfortable seat. He smiled ruefully at Piers who opened up the paper. It helped to keep their faces hidden from view. He made sure that the front page was turned under out of sight. It was a nice sensation travelling incognito in soft, comfortable clothes. Both men were enjoying a quiet sense of elation among the now mostly sleeping travellers.

At Reading they got off the train and jogged out of the town. They went along a country lane for about half a mile where they found a battered vehicle parked on the verge by a field gate. Una greeted them warmly. She drove them to her house without further conversation where David, after being provided with a cup of tea and something to eat, remained on duty outside. This was his own decision but when Una brought him a second cup of tea he said.

'I hope he doesn't do this too often in the winter.'

22~

'What do you know about the ES?' Piers settled himself comfortably in a fireside chair and took a sip of Una's excellent coffee.

'Nothing good,' she said. She was drying her hands and taking off her apron. She came over and sat facing Piers. 'They're filthy rich, racially prejudiced and deeply suspect in several other ways as far as I'm concerned.'

'Have you any actual evidence of them flouting the racial equality convention?'

'No.'

'That's no good then. I need something concrete.'

'Is this about Hugo Finch and his application for a seat in your Parliament?'

'Oh, you know about that?'

'Only because his wife told me.'

'I see.'

'You want to prevent it, I imagine.'

'You can imagine what you like, Una.'

'Bloody diplomat! Are you looking for help to incriminate him?'

'Certainly not. I have whole teams of people to do that if it's necessary. I don't need to put you at risk.'

'It's a matter of risk, then.'

'Everything is a risk when ambitious men want power or money - or both.'

'That's Hugo! He's a quick thinker and a fast talker. I believe many human beings think more slowly today than those of the past.'

'If that's true, what do you believe to be the cause?'

'Several centuries of amplified music, played too loudly for the ears to maintain their proper function. That was partly responsible. You can't think fast if you can't hear properly. Eventually it becomes natural to adopt a slower response. Also, the industrial use of microwaves and other things that are still in use.'

'Go on.'

'Cell phones and watch mechanisms, and cybernetics, the immersion of consciousness in a false dimension. All these things take away the brain's quick functioning and replace it with a slower synaptic response.'

'You've read the research?'

'Yes, and so should you have done. Such things should be discussed at sessions of the World Parliament.'

'They are discussed, of course, but . . .'

'But big business still has a stranglehold on your consumer policies.'

'Una, I've done a lot. Made a lot of changes. I can't do everything at once.'

'You have to be careful who takes a hand in the decision making.'

'I know. Even now I have some doubts about the Council of Electors. It seems possible they may accept Hugo Finch, for instance, and I honestly don't believe he has the right motives. He knows how to say all the right things, that's always been the problem with him and his kind.'

'If you believe he's not genuine you can use your veto.'

'I hesitate to do that if the full Council is in favour. It's not for me to blacken the names of intending MWPs.'

'Can't you do it?'

'The trouble is, I fear I may be prejudiced.'

'But surely you know the man you're talking about better than any of them?'

'Yes, I think I probably do, but I still want to avoid a biased judgement. I wouldn't wish to condemn anyone without clear evidence.'

'Of course not.'

'Lets not talk about him. How's Eden - and little Prune?'

'I haven't seen them for a while Prunella was fine last time she stayed here. I expect she'll be back. Eden gets tired of the responsibility from time to time.'

'How would you feel about having her to live here with you?'

'I could cope. But she adores Eden. She wouldn't be happy if she could never go home to Wimbledon Common - to him and the cats.'

'The cats would fit in here.'

'Steady on, Piers! This is my life we're talking about. I take it you're wanting to get her away from Eden's influence.'

'I think sometimes he puts her in danger.'

'I can't argue with that, but you know, he always sends her off to me if his life gets really complicated.'

'Hmm.' Piers gazed into the fire, enjoying the equality and informality of the conversation.

'Leave them alone, Piers. They've got a way of life worked out. It could be worse.'

'I'd happily pay you to take her.'

'Stop that at once. I'm not swayed by cash. Have you forgotten who you're talking to?'

'Sorry.' Piers put down his coffee mug in the hearth.

'Want a brandy?'

'In a minute, maybe. I'm savouring the after-taste of your coffee.'

'Don't get like those rich manipulators, Piers.'

'I won't.'

'You have such a lifestyle. I don't see how you can avoid being affected by all that - grandeur.'

'I'm not in the job for the grandeur, you know.'

'Darling, I know you're not. But society isn't following your example in that respect. Half the countries of the world may be run in accordance with your political philosophies, but wealth still talks and it makes for the most terrible immorality.'

'Go on.'

'Look at the division between rich and poor! Don't you see how immoral it is for even one person to have a massive income and live in luxury whilst there's even one person hungry or desperate to survive for lack of a few coins. I have nothing against good living, or even wealth that's honestly acquired, but anyone in the world today who lives as an Insider has to be hard enough to care nothing for Outsider conditions, or else they have quite deliberately to turn a blind eye to the inequality.'

'All right, let me play Devil's Advocate. Everyone has the choice. No one has to be an Outsider. If they choose that life they still have an income to ensure they have the basic necessities. I've seen to it that no one needs to starve.'

'You think an Outsider can cross over the divide at will?'

'No, but I don't think your lifestyle's so bad. If you wanted to be an Insider you could do it tomorrow. So could anyone with intelligence and a bit of energy.'

'But I don't want to. I have enough, just enough to live as I do. I don't want more. I don't want my good mind and my fine education numbed by guilt or insensitivity, and that's what would happen if I went and lived in a compound. Oh, I could work as a teacher or a healer. My sort of healing is very popular now. I could make millions if I chose to set myself up in the Chelsea or the H and H. But I don't want that. I want to show people how they could live if they gave up all that greed and status and shit.'

'But anyone could live as you do. Any Outsider could follow your example. That's why I've given them a living allowance. It's a viable alternative to the compounds and one I hoped thousands of people would opt for. Everyone has that opportunity. If they learn a trade and earn a bit extra, they can build their lives up into anything they want.'

'But it hasn't happened, Piers. I think in a way the living allowance may have made things worse. They have their drugs on demand. They have their mind-numbing TV programmes, and their even more mind numbing cyber freak-outs. They don't go to the opera and the theatre like you. They don't come home to beautiful shiny kitchens or houses kept spotless for them. They don't sleep at night in silk sheets and wake up to see their eager little children sitting at their computer terminals and searching the web for the kind of knowledge that will get them the best jobs in the future.'

'Nor do you.'

'No, but I could if I wanted to. Where is their incentive to do better? Most of them are too exhausted to try. Poverty or dependence has become their addiction. I want to see them break it. Better still, I want to see you help them break it.'

'That's why I come here, Una. To have the scales ripped off my eyes. I know these things. Of course I know them, but you're right, I live my life in a lotus land of luxury, and I imagine I can do some good for the poorest people by providing cheap rail travel and keeping the drug pushers off their backs. Tell me where I'm going wrong. Keep telling me. I love you. I value you. - I love you so much.'

'Are you making fun of me?'

'Certainly not. I mean what I say.'

'I'll get the Cognac. I could do with a glass myself.'

Piers got up and began moving about the room, picking things up and putting them down again. Una said, 'Would David like some brandy?'

'What, on duty?'

'You never needed him before when you came here.'

'He never found out before that I was giving him the slip. Now I'm sussed I can't leave him behind.'

'Does he know about Esmeralda?'

'I'm afraid so.'

'I'm going to give him some brandy.'

'Okay.'

He could hear her outside talking to David.

'I can make you a very comfortable bed on the sofa,' she was saying.

'No thanks,' David took his night duty seriously.

'Well, at least come in when we go up to bed.'

'I'll think about it.'

'And drink that,' she said sternly, 'It'll do you good.'

When she came back inside Piers was holding Robin Sheldon's notes for the pylon solar panel scheme.

'What's this?' he said.

'What's what? What are you looking at?'

'An amazingly brilliant plan for solar energy.'

'Oh, that.' She began washing up the coffee mugs.

'Who is Robin Sheldon?'

'Just someone who . . .'

'He won the Nobel some years back, didn't he?'

'You shouldn't need to ask me things like that.'

'I do know him. He's a maverick scientist. An anarchist, like you.'

'I object to that.'

'Did he know I might come here now?'

'I object to that too.'

'All right.'

'For God's sake, Piers.' she turned round from the sink, 'did even I know you might come here now? Months go by and I never see you. I'm not complaining but you can't think I've set you up?'

'I wouldn't put it past you. When did he bring these plans?'

'I don't know. A lot of intelligent people come here and talk to me and show me their plans and their paintings and their poems.'

'But not all of them look capable of cutting the world's energy costs to a fraction of what they are now.'

'Is that what he's offering to do?'

'Yes, Una. You know he is. Where can I get hold of him?'

'His address is probably somewhere on the papers. If you look carefully I expect you'll find it.'

'Don't be so prickly. I'll think you've got a guilty conscience.'

'Oh really! If you want to know, he runs a farm in Warwickshire, a bit like this only five times the size. He's totally self-sufficient. He employs a team of very contented Outsiders too.'

'A man after your own heart.'

'If you say so.'

23~

The Derbyshire children were playing on the grassy plot just inside the Swiss Cottage gates of the Hampstead compound. They liked to play there, preferring it to the little park opposite their home from which they could be seen from the windows by their mother. Of course they had their watches on and the chip in each watch gave an accurate bearing on where a person was and the mini camera in the watches worn by Insider children projected a picture onto the safety screen in their home showing who or what was near them. Nevertheless, they always seemed to wander away towards the gates, despite the fact that they had been told not to play there. Perhaps that was the very reason why the gate area had such an attraction for them. Their father's instruction to stay well inside the compound because it was safe had fallen on deaf ears. They did not want to be safe. They wanted excitement, and in any case they had a friendly relationship with most of the gate guards and were sometimes invited into their gatehouse and allowed to watch the TV screens in their office. Once they had seen their mother on screen, coming out of their house and looking across at the park and then up and down the road for them. They had cheered her delightedly until Lucy's watch had bleeped and their mother's angry voice had issued from it with a curt,

'Where are you?'

'They're with me, Mrs Derbyshire, 'the guard had said.

'Well, send them home at once,' had been their mother's response and the guard had sent them off with a friendly hope that they weren't in too much trouble.

In fact, the Derbyshires had asked the guards to keep a special eye on their children and to discourage them from lingering or playing near the gates. But the guards liked kids and their job was often boring. A couple of bright children could cheer up an hour very pleasantly. But it was always understood, it went without saying, that the children never went outside the gates alone. The guards knew this and the children knew it and that went unquestioned.

Prune was sitting on the grass verge just outside the gates when Lucy and Ben arrived to play near the guardhouse. They had played a game of hide and seek round the trees and hedges and then Ben had ducked in and hidden behind the guardhouse door. As Lucy looked round for him Prune watched her, then she got up and came to the gate and stood looking through the bars with her face pressed against them. After a while Lucy glanced at her and Prune said,

'He's in there,' and pointed at the guardhouse.

Lucy crept over and pounced and Prune roared with laughter as Ben was dragged out. The two children on the inside came to the gate and looked at the childlike creature with the slightly strange round face, peering at them from the other side.

'I've seen you before,' said Ben, trying to remember.

'It was in that cafe at the sea-side,' said Prune.

'That's right,' said Lucy. 'What are you doing here?'

'Waiting for my brother to pick me up.'

'Does he live in here?' asked Ben.

'No, but he . . .'

'I expect he's visiting,' said Lucy, who had realised that Prune was perhaps a little retarded and wanted to make things easy for her.

'Mmmm' said Prune, not knowing what to say.

'You've been waiting ages,' said Ben.

'Would you like to come in,' said Lucy, 'I'm sure the guard wouldn't mind.' At that moment they heard the guard's phone ring and he came out talking into the mouthpiece that was fixed near his cheek.

'Yes, sir I think we have her here,' he was saying, and then to Prune, 'Are you Prunella Diamond?'

'Yes,' said Prune.

'Right, sir,' said the guard, 'I'll keep her here until you can come for her... Don't worry, it's no trouble.' He pressed the switch on his power pack and the pedestrian section of the gate clicked open. 'Come in, young lady,' he said. 'Your brother's delayed and you'll be safe waiting inside until he can get here.'

Prune thanked him and came in. She knew that Eden must have seen her encounter with the Derbyshire children on the receiver from her watch cam. She also knew that he could have contacted her on that if he had wanted to give her a message about a delay. This was a message via the guard, just to get her admitted to the compound. Eden was so clever.

The children played another game of hide and seek with Prune until Lucy's watch bleeped and her mother, having seen on screen the strange little figure her children had encountered, wanted to know what was going on. Lucy went beyond a row of trees and had a whispered conversation with her mother, as a result of which Prune was invited to their house for a meal. She accepted this with a casualness that she believed would have made Eden proud of her and the three of them made their way across the park into the widely spaced prosperous houses, one of which was Ben's and Lucy's home.

24~

Hugo had been born in Dublin and many of his relatives still lived there. He knew a lot about the city. His finance company owned a number of properties there and the rent they brought in was part of the company's income. Since the properties were in an Outsider district it was necessary for an agent to visit Dublin fairly frequently to sort out problems when they arose, such as leaking roof-tiles, unpaid rents or disturbances among the tenants. The houses were in a fairly respectable area and were mainly let to Outsiders who earned their own living one way or another. As long as the rents came in the company avoided asking too searchingly about the tenants' sources of income. One of the tenants, a man named Kenneth Allingham, was running a small group of prostitutes. Among the prostitutes was a rent boy called Jason. Hugo had known Jason's parents when he was a student in Dublin. They had been fairly well off but had held the kind of views that caused them to lose their Insider status when Jason's father was given a prison sentence for breach of the peace over a government measure he disapproved of. This had meant that Jason was pitchforked into Outsider living in his early teens. He had been filled with resentment against his father and against the regime that made him an outcast. His decline into prostitution had been an act of rage and aggression against society and against himself. He carried a knife at all times and the pimp who controlled the house where he lived gave him a wide berth and a lot of latitude.

The agent who looked after the Dublin properties was the man who did most of the finance company's dirty work. He was a very smooth operator. He had studied psychology but had no interest in the clinical aspects of the subject. He was far better off working for a finance house where his trustworthiness, discretion and loyalty gave him the opportunity to name his price for many of the transactions he negotiated. His name did not appear on the company's payroll. He worked as a freelance operator under as many different names as proved convenient. He was always paid in cash and he had a single bank account into which he put a modest amount each month and from which he drew reasonable living expenses. As for the rest it was stashed away in a variety of places, discovery of any one of which revealed no connection with any of the others. He was a respected Insider whose work took him into the Outsider community often enough for him to have a considerable number of hiding places there. He was a man who liked clothes and cars but he did not let his luxurious tastes or his wealth tempt him to extremes. He had lived in a number of compounds where he presented the front of a quiet man of business who socialised superficially but kept himself to himself and caused no one any trouble. He was a man with little or no conscience who greatly enjoyed duping society on behalf of his employers, on his own behalf and on behalf of the Elite Society, for whom, at Hugo's instigation, he often undertook secret missions. His visit to Julia Barton – now Swales - for instance, had been known only to Hugo, to the treasurer, Ian Derbyshire, and to the President. The agent enjoyed working for the Elitists. They paid extremely well and the sense of superiority the assignments carried suited his temperament.

'I want you to go to Ireland tomorrow,' said Hugo.

'More trouble with the Dublin properties?' inquired the agent.

'Not for the moment, no.' Hugo reached into the bottom drawer of his desk and took out a small package. 'You'll find two unused phones in here.'

'Oh yes?'

'I want you to pay a visit to Jason Marn. He lives at . . .'

'I know where Jason lives.'

'Excellent.' Hugo looked very directly at the agent for a moment. The agent's eyes did not waver. Hugo took a minute yellow phone out of the package.

'Give him this and tell him to ring the number installed in it. You will not be able to switch on the phone yourself. It is protected by a password known only to Jason. By the time you reach him he will have been notified of the password.'

'I see.' The agent was smiling.

'He will make the specific call on the phone, for the purpose of which you will ensure that he is confined to a space from which he cannot escape because you hold the key. You will know how to execute this.'

'Indeed.' The agent was still smiling.

'You will not be required to listen to this call or to any calls that Jason makes. You will phone me on the number installed in the second phone when Jason has rung you on his phone to tell you that his specified call is completed. He will know the number of your phone. You will not be given the number of his unless it becomes necessary at any time. The password for your phone is 'cobra'. When you phone to say Jason has rung you I will give you further instructions as necessary. If all has gone well, you will probably be told to retrieve the phone from Jason and simply bring both the phones back to me here where their cards will be removed and destroyed.'

'Understood.' The agent placed the two tiny phones in separate pockets on the inside of his jacket.

'Here is a sum to cover your expenses.' Hugo handed over a fairly fat envelope of bank notes. 'Your payment on return may well amount to more than five times that sum considering the importance of the enterprise.'

'May I ask whether I am working for the company or for the Elite Society on this assignment?'

'Be content that you are working for me. I have no intention of giving you further background at this juncture. This is a very high status assignment. Higher than anything you or I have yet been involved in.' He stood up, so did the agent. He paused a moment and then, half turning to the window said,

'I feel I ought to warn you that Jason is confirmed HIV positive. He is maintained on a fairly costly drug programme but that does not make his bodily fluids any less dangerous.'

'Understood.'

'I don't wish to imply anything by giving you this information but . . .'

'Understood,' said the agent again and the two looked at each other for a moment before shaking hands. Hugo crossed to the door and opened it and the agent departed without further conversation.

When he had gone Hugo rang Ian Derbyshire. Having got through to him he said,

'Ian, I shall need a temporary phone transmitter cell activated on a unique wave band for twenty-four hours from ten hundred hours tomorrow. I want it destroyed on deactivation and rendered completely untraceable. Can you do that for me?' There was a pause before Ian agreed and then Hugo gave the three phone references, including his own and received a link code for the temporary cell. 'You're a technical genius,' he said. There was a moment's laughter and a brief exchange of pleasantries before Hugo rang off, locked his office and set off for home.

25~

'Have some more, Prunella.' Valerie Derbyshire was smiling with her serving spoon poised.

'No, thanks,' said Prune. She had already had two helpings and felt she really couldn't accept any more. She watched the remainder of the dish being scraped onto Ben's plate. He had had more than two helpings now, but he lived here. At home the food was never appetising enough for her to want a second helping and in any case there was hardly ever enough for more than one plateful each. Eden was not much of a cook. They ate out when they could afford it. When they couldn't he made vegetable stews on good days and they had ready-made meals out of tins and cartons the rest of the time. 'It was a lovely meal,' she said. Something wistful in her tone made Valerie say,

'What sort of meals are you used to?'

'Nothing like this,' said Prune. 'This is nearly as good as my godmother's cooking.'

'Oh, really? Thanks very much, I'm assuming that's a compliment.' Valerie sounded not entirely pleased to be outflanked by what might turn out to be an Outsider godmother. 'Where does she live?'

'She has her own farm,' said Prune proudly.

'Oh, real!' said Lucy.

'Where?' said Ben.

'I don't know,' said Prune. 'We go there by car. I know the way, sort of, but I don't know what the address is.'

'In one of the rural compounds, I expect,' said Valerie.

'I don't think it's in a compound,' said Prune. 'You don't have to go through any gates with guards.

'Is your godmother an Outsider?' Lucy asked, fascinated.

'Lucy!' said her mother. 'That is not the sort of question you ask people. What is your godmother's name, Prunella?'

'Una,' said Prune. 'And I'm called Prune. Prunella is just my name for having on printed documents and in my passport.'

'What's your second name?' asked Ben.

'Diamond,' said Prune.

'Like the First Minister,' said Valerie.

'Yes,' said Prune, 'He's my brother.'

'He can't be,' said Ben.

'Real!' said Lucy.

'Don't be silly, dear,' said Valerie, looking at Prune with obvious disapproval.

'No,' said Prune, 'sorry, I should have said half-brother.'

'I don't think you can be telling us the truth,' said Valerie.

'I am!' said Prune with some determination. She got up from her chair and went to where she had left her small holdall. After scrabbling in it for a moment she emerged triumphantly, holding a greetings card with a photograph of Piers in an official line up with various heads of state. On the back was the coat of arms of the World Parliament. Prune brought the card to Valerie and said,

'See!' a little belligerently.

Valerie looked at the card. It read:

Happy Birthday Prune.
Get yourself something nice with the cheque.
Hoping to see you when I'm in the UK in March.
Lots of love, Piers.

26~

'...The Christ himself exhorted his followers to perform, and perform repeatedly, a ritual act of symbolic cannibalism. "Take, eat," He said, "This is my body that is given for you. Do this in remembrance of me." The Christian church has made this the most important of its sacraments, the very centre of its faith. The Roman Catholics actually believe that the word is made flesh as they eat the communion wafer and that they are imbibing the real flesh and blood of Jesus. Be that as it may, all Christians derive much spiritual energy and strength from this ritual of eating part of a man.' Hugo paused and looked at the attentive, intelligent faces in front of him. His lectures to new members were a hallmark of the initiation into the Society. All the listeners were men. All were wealthy and successful. Each one had been approached by a member who knew them well and had succumbed to the excitement of belonging to a secret society, from the safety of whose membership they could look down on the rest of the world. Most of them had been present at the centenary dinner. They were about to learn more about that occasion in retrospect. Smiling, enjoying the attention, Hugo continued: 'And this belief in the power of imbibing flesh is not restricted to the Christians only. The North American Indians believed that eating a man's flesh would uplift them and enable them to perform deeds far beyond the ability of ordinary humans. Sitting Bull, the great chief, whose Indian name was Tatanka Iyotanka, cut strips of flesh from his chest and arms and fed them to his warriors before his last great battle. In this way his spirit entered into the warriors and they were able to fight as never before, uplifted by a superhuman strength.

We, the Elitists, do not believe that such faith is meaningless. We have taken, in essence, the central focus of such teaching and made of it, not a solemn religious rite but a joyous event, a celebration, a feast. That is why, on rare and special occasions, you will be entertained here and given the opportunity to eat the 'tender meat' that we respect and value so highly. I need hardly say that the cost in hard cash is immense, nor do I have to stress to you the fact that we keep this secret as it has always been kept by Elitists of the past. Most people would not be advanced enough in their thinking to understand what we do. Even here the secret of our celebratory meat is only divulged to the most trusted members, like yourselves. The infants involved are, of course, only those who would and could have had no useful life. And we like to think that we are giving a purpose to the occasional and specially chosen little life in carrying it with us, and celebrating it in a way that it might never otherwise have been celebrated - valuing it as it might never otherwise have been valued.'

At this point in the lecture a young man in the second row of the small gathering, who had been present at the centenary dinner, slid unconscious from his chair and crumpled onto the floor. It was considered best for the lecture to come to an end at this point. Each of the listeners, however, was taken for a walk in the beautiful grounds of Pinecott Cedars and encouraged to share their thoughts, one to one, with a long term member of the Society so that they would not be left with any doubts or difficulties relating to what they had heard. In some cases, an extended stay at the house was recommended.

Hugo himself took a walk at this juncture. He liked to keep an eye on the reactions of new members after the lecture. If too many of them seemed upset or likely to be troublesome, he knew he would lose his position as lecturer and he enjoyed the status he derived from this. He would not have been happy to give it up.

'What's with the boy who fainted,' he asked Anthony Partridge who had fallen into step beside him.

'We don't know yet. He may need a few days of special mind-tutoring. He's been put in one of the basement rooms to cool off. He'll soon come to his senses there.'

'They were all carefully vetted before this final initiation lecture.' Hugo was feeling worried.

'I should hope so. We don't want namby-pamby fools joining. I hope you and the selection team are not losing your touch.'

'I doubt that very much, Tony. Half the world will accept almost anything in exchange for a rise in status. And you have to admit, membership of our organisation carries enough prestige to satisfy any serious status seeker.'

'What about the other half of the world? The ones who don't care about status?'

'You don't need to worry about them, surely. They're probably Outsiders. They simply don't count.'

'They count with some people.' The president sounded worried. 'We don't want any bad publicity, Hugo.'

'What - you mean social workers, do-gooders? You've nothing to fear from them. Their opinions are of no value. The press and the media ignore them.'

'I don't have any worries at that level.'

'Who then?'

'Piers Diamond, for instance.'

'Piers Diamond? I don't suppose he loses much sleep over what we do. I imagine we're of very little interest to him. He's the last person who'd ever want to apply for membership, though it might do us some good to have him on board.'

'He wouldn't qualify - the man's a half-caste.'

'You'd be that strict?'

'Certainly I would. Standards are standards, after all.'

27~

It was a beautiful day. The park beyond the window was shimmering in the sun. A small group of children was running to and fro around the trees and bushes. Julia watched them through the blur of her tears. She was wearing her old dressing-gown and finishing a half cold cup of coffee. She had had breakfast late and the young Afro-Caribbean woman who came in to clean the house for her was already in the kitchen making clattering sounds and playing loud music on the music station output. Julia picked up her coffee mug from the spotless white gloss paint of the window-sill where it left a big brown ring. She didn't bother to wipe it off. The woman, who was called Ebbie, a childhood diminutive of Deborah which Julia found irritating, would clean it and render it and every surface in the house spotless. Sometimes Julia imagined herself spraying a great arc of graffiti across one of the tastefully decorated walls, 'I hate you all.' - 'I want my baby.' - 'Let me out.' Better on the outside of the house perhaps. What would they do when they saw it? Put her in a clinic, probably. Would she like that better? It might give her someone to talk to, in the new, carefully enunciated voice that the elocution teacher the Agent had provided had taught her during her pregnancy. They had paid for that too. And who were 'they'? The Agent had brought her here. Her anti-natal appointments schedule and home visits, her dental and hairdresser's appointments and the times of her elocution lessons had been given to her as a print-out. She had attended the appointments dumbly, like an animal, feeling as if she belonged to the peculiarly generous organisation that seemed to be responsible for changing her lifestyle so radically. She could afford a car to take her anywhere she wanted to go in the Insider world. She only had to punch in a number on her carefully Insider-restricted cell phone. But she didn't want to go anywhere, least of all back where she had come from. She could afford to buy any clothes she liked. But she liked her dirty old dressing-gown better than anything. If no one official was coming to see her she would often wear it all day. At first she had got dressed because of Ebbie. She had no doubt that Ebbie would report on her behaviour to whoever it was who had provided all this money and the lovely house. Early on there had been lots of visits from people who wanted to be sure that her pregnancy was progressing according to plan and that she was settling down and feeling contented. Since the birth all that had stopped. There had been no post-natal care. No other mothers to talk to. Nothing. She saw other mothers, walking in twos and threes in the park, pushing baby wheelers, wearing baby packs, sitting together, cuddling their babies, calling out to toddlers, enjoying the safety of the compound's park in the warmth of the sunshine. Julia wanted to howl. Sometimes she did, but not when Ebbie was there.

'Have you finished with your cup, Mrs Swales?' Ebbie was bringing in her up-to-the-minute equipment for germ-free living, prior to turning the room upside down and then setting it straight again. Julia drank the dregs of the cold coffee and held out the mug, 'Yes.'

'That's a nasty ring you made. You are lucky to have this lovely house. I used to have one like it. Don't you go spoiling it. You try to keep it nice for me, won't you?'

'It's my house,' muttered Julia.

'What?' Ebbie paused, about to start her cleaning onslaught. 'Let me run you a nice bath. You've got the very latest jacuzzi up there. If I was you I'd spend half my day in it. I only wish I had the time on my hands that you do. What are you staring at?'

'The park. There are three children playing.'

'And I suppose you think you wish your kiddy was there.' She came and stood next to Julia but not near enough to touch her. 'I understand, but mooning about like this won't help you. Believe me, I know.'

'I think they're playing hide and seek.'

'That older girl is pretty. The boy's a bit chubby. He needs more exercise I guess.'

'The other child's slower off the mark than the other two. Look how kind they are to her, though.' Julia was speaking almost to herself.

'That looks like Down's Syndrome to me.'

'Is it? Is that what it's like?'

'Yes, they never grow up. That little one's probably a lot older than the other two.'

Julia was suddenly blinded by fresh tears.

'Don't you fret, Mrs Swales,' Ebbie said, 'It's no joy to be like that.'

'But...'

'But nothing. You be glad your baby went the way of all flesh before she got old enough to know she was retarded.'

'But I would have loved her.'

'So you might but you wouldn't have had much life hampered by a thing like that.'

'I heard her cry, just once. Then they took her away and a few minutes later they told me she'd died.'

'Best thing. It couldn't have worked out better, for her or for you. You'll get over it.'

'I don't think so.'

'Yes, you will. Don't stand there looking at that kid, it's morbid. Get yourself dressed up nice and smart and go out up to the heath. You can look at the shops on the way and if you go to the High Heath Bar you might meet a nice man and, who knows, given a bit of time you might get married again.'

'I don't want to be married. It's the last thing I want.'

'What happened to your husband?'

There was a knowingness in Ebbie's tone.

'I don't want to talk about it.'

'Same as mine, I expect.' Julia looked at Ebbie and felt suddenly frightened.

'Okay, okay.' Ebbie turned away, 'I'll get on. You should get dressed. It would make you feel better.'

They had given her a wedding ring and filled out all her information sheets as Mrs Swales. Her name had actually been changed to Mrs Julia Swales by deed poll. The house was in that name. She had been told to refuse to talk about Mr Swales, whoever he might be supposed to have been. He was simply and respectably dead. You could not live in a commune as an unmarried mother. Terminated marriage was socially impossible if a child had been conceived. Temporary marriages were accepted only among those who had taken temporary vows and had no intention of having children. Pregnancy meant that the vows must, by law, be made permanent. Birth-control was perfectly simple and totally reliable. There was no such thing as an unmarried mother among Insiders.

28~

The Derbyshires were getting to like Prune and it would never have occurred to them not to trust her. Eden wanted information on the Elite Society that Ian, as their treasurer, would be bound to have documented somewhere. He had certain information already but he knew there was more and he needed concrete proof. Prune had been carefully placed in the bosom of the family and he now needed to elicit the necessary facts through her by ensuring that she asked the right questions without knowing what she was asking. He knew she would chat about whatever topic he had recently discussed with her so, on the morning of the day when she had been invited to their house they talked about safes. He told her what she had never needed to know before, that a safe had a combination and explained the basics of a combination lock to her.

'So, have we got a safe?' Prune asked.

'No,' said Eden. 'But Piers has one and guess what the combination is.'

'I don't know,' said Prune sulkily. She hated questions that caught her out.

'He uses the date of your birthday; the year, the month and the day, to make sure he remembers how to get the door open.'

'And that's how he always remembers my birthday too,' said Prune.

'Exactly,' said Eden.

Prune was very happy to join in Lucy and Ben's games and she introduced them to one of her own. It was the game where you throw a ball over the roof and run through the house to try and catch it on the other side. They played this for about half an hour when she first introduced it. The game was a great success with Lucy and Ben, neither of whom had ever thought of such a thing and neither of whom could do it very easily. Prune couldn't do it either but she could see that Ben was getting the hang of it.

'Why can't we do it?' Prune said to Lucy, when they had both tried in vain while Ben developed that same flick of the wrist that she had seen Eden and Piers give the ball.

'I expect it's a 'boy thing',' said Lucy sarcastically. She was getting bored with it when she found she couldn't do it easily. Ben sent another ball sailing over and all three of them dashed through, jostling each other and falling over and roaring with laughter because they had all missed the ball. Valerie Derbyshire came out and told them to stop the stampeding.

'Play quietly,' she said.

'Piers Diamond used to play this game,' said Ben. 'Prunie told us about it.'

'Well I'm sure he doesn't do it now, and nor can you,' said Valerie. 'Go and wash your hands now. It's nearly time to eat.'

The Derbyshires were all at the dining table when Prune announced her newly acquired information on safes. Her lecture on the subject was lengthy and, since she had never actually seen a safe it was not entirely accurate. Ian Derbyshire, finding this diatribe rather annoying and being, as always, unable to resist putting someone right, said curtly, 'There's a safe in my study, I'll show it to you after supper if you like.'

'Wow, yes. Real!' said Prune who had learnt the word from Lucy and thought it was the height of sophistication.

'Come on,' said Ian when the meal was over. He and Lucy, Ben and Prune went across the hallway to the study.

'Piers uses the date of my birthday for the combination of his safe,' said Prune proudly.

'That's funny,' said Lucy, 'Dad uses my birth date for his.' She spoke the numbers in a sing-song voice, '21-04…'

'Stop!' shouted her father. In front of the Picasso print that concealed the safe he had turned abruptly to face the children.

'Lucy, Prunella,' his face was far from friendly, 'do you realise how much harm you could do by blurting out that information. You must never, either of you, utter the facts that you have just told us. Fortunately, no one is here who would use the information wickedly, but someone could. Prune, for instance, if she wanted to, could break into my safe and steal all sorts of things and I, for instance, if I wanted to, could now break into the safe of the First Minister of the World Parliament.'

'No you couldn't,' said Prune, 'Because you don't know my birthday.'

Later that evening, over a mug of hot chocolate, a treat that Eden usually reserved for very special occasions because chocolate was so expensive, Prune proudly informed him that the first four digits of Ian Derbyshire's safe combination were 21-04; his daughter's birth date.

'I couldn't get the rest,' she said sadly 'He shouted at her to shut up.'

'I bet he did,' said Eden. 'And how old is Lucy?'

'Fourteen,' said Prune.

'Are you sure about that?'

'Yes, she was fourteen in April. She told me last time I was there.'

'What a bit of luck.' Eden was smiling.

'Is fourteen lucky?'

'Very lucky, Prune. Very lucky indeed!'

'Good,' said Prune. After a pause and the disappearance of some of the chocolate drink she said, 'Do you know what he keeps in his safe?'

'No.'

'Ha ha! I know and you don't.'

'Are you going to tell me?'

'If you ask really nicely.'

'Please, Prune tell me what Mr Derbyshire keeps in his safe.'

'Mm-mm.' Prune pressed her lips together and shook her head.

'Dear Prune, pretty Prune, please tell me. I should so much like to know.'

'You really want to know about his safe, don't you?'

'Yes, I do. He's a man who interests me.'

'Well, don't get so interested in him that we have to never see them again, like usually happens 'cos I like Ben and I really like Lucy. She's real!'

'Oh, Prune, what a life I give you. I'm really sorry but sometimes, you know...'

'Well, he doesn't have anything bad in his safe. He has jewels.'

'Does he? What kind of jewels?'

'Knobbly ones.'

'What?'

'Uncut... er, jams he said they are. Lots of them in a blue velvet bag with the velvet on the inside. He says they're worth a small fortune. That's the only reason why he has to have a safe.'

'I see. I think you mean 'gems'.'

'Are we going to steal them? I could get them and we could be rich.'

'No, Prune. That would put an end to a beautiful friendship. Don't even think about that. Don't let me hear you say such a thing again.'

Prune finished her chocolate quickly, spilling a little down her front. It was one of her favourite treats. Eden knew this and she was afraid that she was losing favour and might have it taken away.

29~

The boy was tall, a little above average height. He had dark hair which was straight and shiny and looked well cared-for. A lock of it hung over his forehead and shaded his eyes. He had large, dark eyes. The light reflected in them offered an attractive suggestion of admiration and slight self-deprecation. Leaning as he was with one elbow on the parapet, he could have been a rent-boy, but the designer clothes and the whisper of wealth about him dismissed any such thought. Piers was walking towards his Geneva residence and the boy was looking at him. Not staring, just looking, and seeming to wait for Piers to draw level with him. He seemed to give off in equal measure both masculine assurance and feminine charm. Piers could not have failed to notice him. He returned the boy's look and the boy did not look away. His eyes held Piers' with a mingled expression of wonder and faint amusement. The bodyguards moved in slightly. As they did so the boy turned and leaned both elbows on the parapet behind him. He looked both casual and vulnerable. One of the bodyguards moved in front of Piers and indicated with a gesture that the boy should be elsewhere. The boy stood up straight. He said something to the bodyguard but it was too quiet for anyone else to hear. He was looking across the man's shoulder at Piers. The man put his hand on the boy's arm as if to follow up his suggestion with a little compulsion. His gun was out.

'It's all right,' Piers said, 'I think the young man wants to speak to me.'

'This is very unorthodox, sir. It would be wiser to have him make an official appointment.' David had come up close to Piers. He knew his advice was correct. So did Piers, and yet, in this incident he saw a pattern of protection that kept him from speaking to ordinary people, befriending them and understanding what they were thinking. He also knew that a boy like this, with no obvious diplomatic credentials, wouldn't have a hope in hell of getting an appointment to see him. He wanted, on an impulse, to talk to this boy at this moment.

'It's all right,' he said quietly to David, 'I intend to find out what he wants to say.'

'He hasn't been vetted, sir.'

'To hell with that!'

'He hasn't even been searched.'

'Then search him if you must.'

They searched him. He held out his arms like Christ and smiled throughout the little ritual. It was quickly done. He had no gun, no knife, no weapon of any kind. David came back to Piers.

'This could be very unwise, sir.'

'I think it's more unwise to be permanently unavailable.'

'As you wish.' He advanced towards the young man, his hand on his gun. Piers put a hand on his shoulder,

'David, it's all right. I'm sure we have nothing to fear from this young man.' David stopped and turned, speaking very quietly.

'Do you know him, sir?'

'No, but I'm sure he knows me. He's taken the trouble to come here. I can take a little trouble on my side and make him welcome.'

The boy's eyes lit up with pleasure and something that could only be described as mischief. He was enjoying the situation immensely. He held out his hand to Piers.

'Mr Diamond,' he said. His voice was husky with a slight Dublin accent. 'I'm honoured to meet you. Really honoured.'

'What can I do for you?' said Piers.

'Do? Nothing. Do you never just meet people and have a chat?'

'That is something that hardly ever happens to me now.'

'Isn't that a sad thing?' said the boy.

'Yes,' said Piers, 'I hadn't realised until today what a sad thing it is.' He began to walk with the boy at his side along the path and onto the wide lawn at the back of the residence. The boy strolled with his hands in his pockets. He was as natural as a young prince might have been, walking beside an elder statesman. A pleasurable sense of being treated as an equal lifted Piers' heart.

'What are you doing in Geneva?' he asked.

'Running away,' said the boy.

'What are you running from?'

'Myself, probably.'

'You look like somebody who is very comfortable with himself.'

'That may be so, but I got in with a few of the wrong people and now I have to find myself again after it.'

'I see.' Piers did not know quite what to say.

'I'm having a sort of holiday,' the boy went on.

'And then you'll be going back to Ireland?'

'Ah, you recognised the brogue. Yes, I imagine I will, although I'd like to live somewhere else for a change. I want to break new ground.'

'What sort of new ground?'

'I'd like to be an actor.'

'Really? Theatre or film?'

'Both - either.'

'You have to train for that.'

'I know. But at the moment I've got a course to finish at Dublin University.'

'What's your subject?'

'Political History.'

'So you're not only committed to being an artist.'

'I don't know what I'm committed to. I need something to believe in and someone to believe in me. My parents have given up.'

'That's a pity. I think I'd be rather proud of a son like you.'

'Listen - could I talk to you again? You're so knowledgeable. Everything I've ever heard you say or do was incredibly wise. I would value it so much if we could talk again.'

Piers looked into the darkly sincere gaze and wanted to help.

'What's your name?' he asked.

'Patrick,' said the boy, 'Patrick Sinclair.'

'Come tomorrow, Patrick. I can give you a little while in the afternoon. Come here, not to the Government building, and we'll have a cup of tea and a chat. I'm off the next morning on a plane to New York and when I get back my schedule's packed. I won't be available again for God knows how long. It was a lucky chance you spoke to me today.'

'It certainly was,' said Jason, 'Thank you so much.'

30~

The next time Prune and the children were playing out in the park, Julia got dressed quickly and went out to be near them. She sat on a bench under the tree nearest to her gate and when she saw them running about and laughing she laughed too. She could see that the Down's child was wearing a watch and after a while, when she was nearer than the others Julia called out to her.

'Excuse me, could you tell me the time?'

Prune came towards her, looking at her watch,

'It's four twenty-eight,' she said.

'Sorry, I didn't quite hear you.'

Prune came closer.

'Four twenty-eight,' she said emphatically.

'That's a nice watch,' said Julia.

'My brother gave it to me,' Prune said proudly.

'You've been running about a lot. Come and sit down and have a little rest.'

Julia patted the bench next to her and Prune came over a little hesitantly and sat as far from Julia as possible. Julia looked at her for a moment wondering what to say. Eventually she asked, 'Are you happy?' It sounded a ridiculous question the moment she had said it but it was the one thing she really wanted to know.

'Yes, thank you,' said Prune politely.

'Do you live here? Are those children your brother and sister?'

'Oh, no,' said Prune. 'They're just people I visit. My proper brother is a grown-up. I live with him. And I've got another brother - a half-brother.'

'Does he live with you too?'

'No.' Something made Prune cautious for once. 'He lives abroad most of the time,'

'And what about your parents?'

'They're dead,' said Prune.

'Oh, I'm so sorry,' said Julia.

'It's all right. I don't mind.'

'Don't you?'

'No. I never knew my mother. She died when I got born and my father was old. I like Eden better. I like Valerie too. She's Ben and Lucy's mum. She's very nice to me. I don't like Ian much - he's their dad. I don't like men, except Eden.'

'Eden?'

'My brother.'

'I see. My name's Julia - what's your name?'

'Prunella. But everyone calls me Prune.'

'Do you mind that?

'What?'

'Being called Prune?'

'No. I like it. I've got to go. It's tea-time. Bye.' She ran off suddenly to catch up with Lucy who was walking towards home.

'Come and have tea with me sometime.' Prune stopped and turned, surveying Julia for a moment, 'I live just here. 'Julia said, indicating her gate. Prune stood for a moment more, perhaps weighing up what Julia might provide for tea, then she ran on without a word. Julia watched her catch up with Lucy whose hand she took as if a taller person's protection was something she took for granted. They went into one of the large houses on the opposite side of the park. Julia wondered what she could do to get to know Prune better and to help to make up for what seemed a rather fragmented life. And yet Prune had said she was happy. That was more than Julia could claim for herself.

31~

Jason Marn presented himself at the residence promptly the next afternoon. His identity card and papers, which were in the name of Patrick Sinclair, had already been checked and returned to him but David insisted on confiscating them while he remained in the building. The photo, name, places of origin and work together with the DNA profile incorporated in the card's information cell had all been verified with the central register and yet David felt a niggling doubt. He ran the check again himself. He even checked with the university department records to ensure that the boy was listed as a former student of Political Philosophy. It all tallied. The international student records produced a picture of a dark haired young man, as like the owner of the documents as anyone might expect in a computer picture, when the appropriate name was entered. The university confirmed by X-mail that Patrick Sinclair had been a student. They did not know that he had intended to approach the First Minister but they did not see anything to be worried about in the event. And still David felt anxious.

Piers invited the young man to sit down and offered him tea, coffee or something stronger. Jason refused refreshment. They talked for a while a little awkwardly and then Jason began to ask questions about Piers' work. He was very interested in the Council of Electors. This was a subject close to Piers' heart and he waxed lyrical on the security of having such a thorough body of reliable men and women, able to ensure that no one could be elected to the World Parliament unless they were a person of absolute integrity.

'But I understand you have the final veto,' said Jason.

'Yes. In the case of any difficult decision I can instruct the Council, or if their votes are equally divided on an issue my vote carries the day.'

'Is that right, do you think?'

'I hope so. After all I have to administer the Parliament in relation to the outcome of these decisions. And they are an advisory body. They're not elected members of the World Government.'

'But it gives you ultimate power and everyone knows that power corrupts.'

'A telling point,' said Piers, 'but in actual fact it does nothing of the sort. There are many checks and balances to curb my powers. And in any case I'm not interested in power, only in progress. When I find someone who knows more than I do on a subject, I listen. When I discover someone wiser than myself, I learn. I am not interested in being obeyed or being 'right', I am only interested in what is good for humanity on a world scale and in the long term.'

'So you have to make many decisions that make you unpopular in the short term, I suppose.'

'Fewer now than were necessary at first.'

'Did you worry at first about making changes that would make you unpopular?'

'If I had ever worried about being popular I would have been totally unfit for the task.'

'The leading ministers of most nations have shamelessly courted popularity in the past.'

'And foolish decisions, wars and riots have often resulted.'

'Do you believe that your premiership has left all that behind?'

'I wouldn't take so much upon myself, but I have written about all this quite extensively and governments throughout the world seem to have taken on my ideas and implemented them quite successfully.'

'You use the word quite in a very modest way. Is all this modesty just another way of ensuring your popularity? After all, you are the most powerful man in the world.'

'I'm not sure whether that question comes from cynicism or lack of trust. I am what you see. I have stood up to a lot of global scrutiny. I think you'll find that other people have already disproved what you are suggesting and have come to trust me. Are you hoping to prove them wrong? Now, isn't it time we talked about you?'

'I . . . I wonder if it would be possible to talk to you alone.'

Piers looked over his shoulder.

'David? Would you leave us for a bit?'

'No, sir.'

'I'm sorry,' said Piers, shrugging his shoulders. 'The rules are the rules.'

'I think I'll accept that drink now, if the offer's still open.' Jason's face looked suddenly very sulky. Piers went to the drinks cabinet and offered a range of possibilities.

'Do you have a single malt?'

'I do,' said Piers. 'Ice?'

'No, I'll take it as it comes.'

While they sipped their drinks and continued to talk David opened the door and called to a member of his team. As soon as Jason's glass was empty he cleared it and went away, leaving his colleague on guard with Piers and the boy. It was a matter of minutes before the DNA sample from the glass had been processed and compared with the sample on the identity card. They did not match. The card belonged to an exemplary student of Political History at the university of Dublin. The DNA from the whisky glass belonged to a very different student who had been thrown off the Art Course after a conviction for soliciting in the street. David returned to Piers' private sitting-room. The boy had gone.

'Where did he go?' David was panting slightly.

'He's just down the corridor. He went to the lavatory.' David issued instructions and the second bodyguard moved fast. Both men had their guns out.

'What's the matter?' Piers was not unused to such events but he was surprised on this occasion.

'He's not Patrick Sinclair. He's Jason Marn, a rent boy from Dublin with a criminal record and he's HIV positive. Unless we act quickly and discreetly you are totally compromised.'

They were gone in an instant and Piers heard no sound except a slight scuffle on the stairs. When David came back half an hour later it was to say,

'The boy's in custody and he'll be interrogated in the morning when he's had time to calm down.'

'What was the purpose, I wonder?'

'To discredit you. Were there any photographers about when you were talking to him yesterday?'

'No. I'm sure not. We were on the back lawn most of the time.'

'It would only take one.'

'I know.'

'The problem is what to do with him. How can we ever trust him if we release him?'

'What other alternative have you in a civilised world?'

'You have to leave this to me, Piers. First we have to find out who sent him here.'

'I could hazard a guess but it would be nothing more than that.'

'Hazard then. We'll check it out very carefully.'

'I know you will but I'd rather leave it until after you've talked to him.'

David laughed wryly,
'This is even worse than Esmeralda getting out!'
'At least Esmeralda can't talk.'

32~

'What news of Jason?'

'Forget him. You don't want to know.' David shook his head.

'Have you questioned him?'

'Not yet. We let him cool his heels overnight and this morning, when he started throwing his breakfast about and yelling, we let him cool off and then offered him a phone to make a call.'

'And?'

'He phoned his pimp - or perhaps I should say his landlord.'

'Anyone we know?'

'No. A man called Allingham, Kenneth Allingham.'

'In Dublin?'

'Yes.'

'Any criminal record?'

'You mean, apart from running a string of prostitutes? We're looking into it. Someone will have to ask Allingham some questions. I don't suppose either he or the boy had a personal motive for discrediting you. Very big money was probably their incentive. I'm pretty sure there's someone else behind this. It's not just a rent-boy and his pimp.'

'When will you let the boy go?'

'Piers, we can't do that. He only has to whisper a word of being here and having a private interview with you and it'll make it world news. You'd be finished.'

'But you were with us all the time. We only talked!'

'I know that and you know that but the world's press will only be interested in his 'profession'! The fact that you talked to him when he approached you outside was one conversation too many. To have invited him in was disaster.'

'So what will you do?'

'Don't ask.'

'You mean he'll disappear.'

'I don't know yet. Maybe.'

'His freedom or his life set against my job. I can't condone that.'

'It's too late for discussing what can or can't be condoned. A rent-boy with AIDS? How much good is he going to do for the future of the world? We certainly can't let him go home and write his memoirs.'

'But he's committed no crime.'

'No, but he's let himself be made the pawn of someone who wants to.'

'Character assassination is not a crime, David.'

'Libel and slander are.'

'There's been none of that yet.'

'You want us to wait until there is? By then it'll be much too late.'

'I don't suppose he knew what he was letting himself in for.'

'I doubt if he knew the degree of harm he could do simply by speaking to you. But he's not stupid. He didn't think he was coming here just to challenge you to a philosophical discussion. Somebody sent him, that's obvious. You have a very clever and very dangerous enemy out there, Piers.'

'I probably have hundreds of enemies. Every good or necessary policy for change inconveniences someone, you know.'

'Yes, but they don't all seek this kind of revenge. You said you had an idea who it might be. Are you going to give me a name?'

'Not yet. Follow up the boy's contacts first. I'd like to wait and see if the name comes up. If it does I'll tell you.'

33~

The whole family was in bed and asleep when Hugo knocked at the door. Valerie woke Ian who was sleeping heavily and, protesting sleepily, he went downstairs, opened the door and stared grumpily at Hugo who was standing there with a bulging briefcase under his arm.

'I need your help. Let me come in,' Hugo said urgently.

'What's the time?' said Ian, still annoyed at being woken.

'About one-thirty,' said Hugo, pushing past him into the hall and shutting the door.

'You make free with your friends.' Ian was speaking tetchily.

'Ian, I'm in trouble - we're all in trouble if I don't get this stuff out of my house.'

'So you bring it here! Thanks very much!' Hugo had made his way into the study uninvited. He switched on the desk-lamp and put his briefcase down on Ian's desk. Ian followed him, yawning. Hugo was speaking quickly and quietly.

'A plan I had to help my application to the World Parliament may have gone wrong. I need to put some papers in your safe until the trouble blows over.'

Ian was gradually coming to his senses.

'Something to do with the recent phone arrangements is it?'

'You could say that.'

'Well, go on. You don't expect me to agree to this blindly, do you? What am I being asked to cover up?'

'Just the deeds of my Dublin properties and the documents relating to their tenancies.'

'Why?'

'One or two of the properties are Outsider brothels. Satisfied now?'

'No. I don't see why that's suddenly an issue. So - you get part of your income in this dubious way. It doesn't make you a criminal.'

'Ian! I'm being investigated by the Council of Electors!'

'Well, they'll find out a thing like this. They can get access to god-knows-what records.'

'But there's nothing on the web relating to this. I've kept it all in paper format. The rents are very carefully laundered through Isabel's bank account. There'll be absolutely nothing for them to find once all the papers are in your safe.'

'You really think they search people's houses? I'm sure they have much better means of finding out about their applicants, means that are far more thorough.'

'Ian, you may be right but I want to play safe. Do you want me to get a seat in the Parliament or don't you?'

'Of course I do. It's high time one of us was in there, but I think all this cloak and dagger stuff seems ridiculous. Is there something you're not telling me?'

'I've said all I'm going to say. If you can't help me, I'll go to Partridge. I'm sure he'll understand.' He picked up the briefcase. The threat of his uncooperative attitude being reported to Partridge disturbed Ian as nothing in the conversation had done so far.

'All right,' he said, going to the safe and getting it open. 'Give me the papers.' Hugo took two large folders out of the briefcase and handed them to Ian. 'Don't worry, I shan't read them. I won't have time'

'Read all you like. It's just a lot of conveyancing documents, tenancy agreements and deeds. I imagine the stuff you keep in there is far more incriminating.'

'Incriminating to the Elitist Society, you might say.'

'We've begun to finance a few deals recently that would put you inside and then Outside for life, Ian.'

'I'm only the Treasurer. I may sign the cheques but I don't broker the deals.'

'You'd sell Partridge and the lot of us down the river, would you, if serious matters came to light?' He put on a namby-pamby voice, 'I only signed the cheques. I didn't know what they were for.'

'It's very late, Hugo,' Ian said, 'don't you think we'd both better get some sleep?'

'Yes.' Hugo smiled his superior smile. 'I'm going.' They went to the door in silence.

'Don't bother to thank me!' said Ian with suppressed outrage as Hugo was about to walk away.

'No. I'm confident I'll have the chance to return the compliment one day,' Hugo murmured between smilingly clenched teeth. Ian watched him turn towards the gates. He wondered what lie this man had told the guard to get himself admitted at this hour. He hoped it was nothing that would make him or any member of the family look foolish.

34~

Prune was growing to hate Ian Derbyshire more and more. She loved Lucy and Ben and she liked their mother but her hatred for Ian was increasing every time she visited the house. Valerie saw how it was but she could do nothing to ease the situation. Ian was constantly sarcastic to Prune and sometimes commented on her naive remarks by repeating them sarcastically. This was not always fully understood by Prune but she knew that she was being attacked in some way and the defensive reaction of the children confirmed this. Valerie's kindness also increased and, since Prune had no mother, she responded very warmly to Valerie.

Prune often stayed overnight with the Derbyshires these days. Sometimes for several days. Eden was often busy and at times when she would once have stayed with Una to get her out of his way she now stayed with the Derbyshires. Eden had encouraged this. He was now waiting for the arrangement to bring him the opportunity he was looking for.

Prune had strict instructions to let him know if she was ever left alone in the house. The likelihood of this was very slight but, if it should happen, a plan was in place. And, with the unpredictability of life, it happened on a Saturday when the children's grandmother was suddenly taken ill and Valerie, Ian and Ben rushed off to see her. They left Lucy at home because she had recently been in a collision in a friend's car and was not supposed to travel in a car again until her neck muscles had recovered from their injury. Naturally Prune stayed with her since Lucy needed company and Prune had no place at the grandmother's bedside. The car had hardly gone out of earshot when Lucy got up from the sofa where she was supposed to be resting and informed Prune that she was going to see Vanda, the friend in whose parent's car the collision had taken place.

'She's much worse off than me,' Lucy said. 'Her collar-bone was broken. I'm going round there, it's very close. And you're to say nothing to Mum or Dad. I'll be back long before they get home. Do you understand? You say nothing about this, ever!'

'Got it,' said Prune.

'Real!' said Lucy and was gone.

This was the eventuality Eden had prepared her for. Prune sent him the agreed text on her mobile and then sat herself down at the kitchen table to a large bowl of chocolate ice-cream from the freezer. She knew a lot about where things were kept in the Derbyshire house.

The gate guard looked at Eden's credentials and let him in. He was going to visit Julia. He had made the appointment by phone as soon as he had received Prune's message and Julia had informed the gate, in the customary way, so that only a brief check was necessary for her visitor on arrival. Prune was not looking out of the window and watching for Eden yet. She was enjoying a second helping of ice-cream. Eden went up the steps and rang Julia's doorbell and was shown into her spick and span sitting-room by Ebbie. When Julia came in they sat down and looked at each other. Julia was scared and Eden was waiting for Ebbie to go. As this was not happening he said,

'I would like to talk to you alone, if that's possible.'

'Of course,' said Julia. 'Ebbie, would you mind?' She looked at Eden, 'Would you like some coffee?'

'No thanks.' He stood up and looked out at the Park. 'What I'd really like is to go out there for a bit. Could you get dressed so that we could go for a little walk?'

'I suppose . . . Yes, all right.'

'I'll wait here. There's no rush.' While he waited he wandered into the spotless kitchen and exchanged a few words with Ebbie. It was not a long conversation but it told him enough to realise that Julia was being watched and that Ebbie was reporting on her state of health and behaviour to the clinic where her baby had been delivered.

'Are you employed by the clinic?' Eden asked.

'I'm employed by the ES,' said Ebbie proudly, 'They pay better than anyone.'

'The Elite Society?'

'Yes.'

'Have you worked for them for long?'

'Quite a while.'

'Do they provide you with accommodation?'

'Yes.'

'Like this?' He indicated the surroundings.

'It used to be a house like this. Now it's an apartment.'

'Why the change?'

'That's their choice. They've done a lot for me.'

110

'Why?'

'Generous, I guess, or they like me. I tell them things they want to know without any fuss.'

'What do they want to know?'

'How Mrs Swales is keeping.... How much she gets out. . ...

'Who visits her?'

'Yes, that too.'

'So you'll tell them about me.'

'Yes.'

'Well, I'm here to cheer her up.'

'She needs that.'

'I know.'

Julia came down stairs looking clean and tidy. She had put on some makeup and her hair was tied up in a wispy knot. She looked at Eden with suspicion as he came out of the kitchen. He said nothing and they walked out across the park away from the house, away from the gates and away from the Derbyshire's house.

'Are you happy with Ebbie,' Eden asked, kindly.

'I don't know,' said Julia. 'She's so terribly spotless and tidy in her standards. She kind of watches me.'

'Not what you were used to in your old life.'

'You know about that.'

'Yes,'

'Why are you here?'

'To help if I can.'

'Is it possible? My baby... could you help me to get her back?'

'No. I can't do that.'

'But I don't know where she is. If I only knew that she was safe.'

'Were you paid a lot of money, Julia?'

'Not just money - the house, the lifestyle - everything.'

'Do you know who paid you?'

'No. A man arranged it all. He arranged for an elocution teacher and ante-natal visits and everything.'

'And now?'

'Nothing. I only see Ebbie these days. You're my first visitor for ages.'

'Do you know the name of the man you mentioned who made the arrangements for you?'

'No.'

'How was the money transferred to you?'

'It's in investments mainly, and there was a whacking big cheque.'

'Do you remember whose signature was on the cheque?'

'Someone called Derbyshire, I think. I remember because of the Peak District. I saw pictures of it once. It looked beautiful. The Peak District of Derbyshire. I wanted to go there.'

'That's what you wanted when you were living in the commune?'

'Yes. I'm not really an Insider, you know. I don't think I'm any happier here, in fact I think I'm more miserable. But I met this little girl called Prune. I watch her out there playing. That cheers me up. The baby I lost would have been like her.'

Eden looked at her intently for a moment and then suggested that they turn and go back. They did so, still keeping above the line of trees and bushes that would shield them from the houses across the park until they almost reached her gate. Eden left her there and said that he hoped to be back again and would help her if he could.

'I understand more than you think,' he said. 'Don't talk about my visit. I shall see you again if and when I can.'

'What is your name?' she asked.

'Gareth,' he said.

'Thank you, Gareth.' She was gone into the house without looking back.

Eden skirted the park behind the trees and came round to the Derbyshire's house. He rang the bell and Prune came to the door. She had chocolate all round her mouth.

'Hello, Prune,' he said, pushing past her and closing the door quickly.

'Hi,' she said, 'What do you think of this then?' She waved a proud hand as if the house were her own.

'Go and wash your face,' he said.

When she came back he was in Ian's study with the safe open. The photocopier was switched on and Eden was running papers through it swiftly and putting them in his briefcase. She watched him do this for about twenty minutes, listening all the time for the sound of the family or Lucy returning.

'You'd be quicker,' she said, 'if you took your gloves off.'

Eden completed his task in silence and then replaced the original papers in the safe, swung it shut, replaced the picture and closed his case.

'I was never here. Understand? I haven't been here. You haven't seen me.'

'Alright. Do you want some ice-cream?'

'No.'

'No what?'

'No thanks!'

'Better! - It's chocolate.'

'I could tell.'

He was gone out of the door and out of sight among the trees before she had time to call out goodbye. She wondered why he was going that way when the gate was in the other direction. She wondered why he hadn't suggested taking her home.

35~

The man came back unexpectedly in the late afternoon. Ebbie had gone and Julia was alone and when she answered the door a chill went through her at the sight of him. She had no idea why, since he was responsible for her whole new lifestyle and she ought to have been glad to see him. She took him into the spotless sitting-room and offered him tea which he refused. She sat down and he sat down and she looked at him dumbly while a growing sense of dread seemed to grip her throat.

'Are you all right?' he asked.

'Yes,' she said, and as she said it tears sprang up in her eyes.

'Ah,' he said, 'you miss your baby.'

'Yes,' she said, sounding weak and pathetic to her own ears.

'I wondered,' he said, shifting himself to a more relaxed position in the chair,

'if you'd like to have another?'

'You mean ...?'

'For us. As you did before. There are so many babies needed. You would be doing a great service.'

'I'd want to keep it,' she said.

'I'm afraid I wouldn't advise that. Your circumstances prohibit it, don't they?'

'Wouldn't they prohibit me from being seen to be pregnant then?'

'Well, you wouldn't be seen here, obviously.'

'Where would I go?'

'After the artificial insemination you would have to be moved to another compound, up country, where no one knew anything about you.'

'Start all over again?'

'Yes - a nice new house - a new name - another completely fresh start. You might like it even better than here.'

'I don't like it much here.'

'Well, there you are then.' He made an expansive gesture. 'It would be just what you need.'

'I'm not giving up another baby.'

'Then I'm afraid you won't be able to be maintained at this standard of living, my dear.'

'What?'

'These houses are not given free, gratis and for nothing to women who are only prepared to offer us one baby.'

'You're going to send me back to an Outsider commune?'

'Certainly not, we shall never do that, but we do hope . . . I personally hope that you will see sense about this and co-operate.'

'You mean I'm trapped into having babies for you or ... what?'

'Well, you could do some other work for us I suppose, cleaning, office work.'

'And where would I live?'

'In one of our apartment blocks.'

'Where?'

'Near your place of work.'

'Would I still be provided for?'

'You'd work and your wages would be fair. You wouldn't live in luxury like this. Only the baby mothers are given this sort of privileged treatment.'

'But I don't want to leave here.'

'I thought you said you were unhappy here.'

'I have been, but there are one or two things that make life worth living.'

'Perhaps we can transfer or replicate those.'

Thinking of Prune and of Gareth Julia shut her mouth and waited to see what he would say next. She had no intention of telling him how much the sight of Prune, happily playing in the park, had kept her from despair. There had been moments when she had thought about killing herself. In another place, with another baby growing inside her that she would have no contact with beyond the day of its birth, she believed that she might well prefer to die once the baby was delivered.

'I'll leave you to think about it.' The Agent got up and stood looking down at her. She had a terrible sense of his having done this with dozens, perhaps hundreds of women. She felt trapped. She wanted to scream. She wanted to beat her fists in his face, to make him bleed and cower and die. She stood up shakily and he steadied her with a hand under her elbow.

'I'm trapped, aren't I?' she said.

'No!' He spoke with a big, reassuring inflection of the voice. 'You mustn't think like that. It's all much easier than you're making it. Enjoy life. Enjoy the prospect of starting afresh. It could all be fun!'

'Not for me,' said Julia. 'And not always for the babies either.'

'Well, that's something we can never know.'

'Is my baby happy, do you think? Do you know what happened . . .?'

'Your baby died, Julia. I'm so sorry. So very sorry, but it's better that you know the truth, I think.'

Standing at the door Julia watched him go down the path and out of the gate. In the park beyond Prune was running after Ben and calling his name. Ben was taking no notice of her. Julia watched with tears coursing down her face until the man and the children were out of sight.

When Ebbie came the next morning Julia had not slept and she was still very tearful.

'What's the matter?' Ebbie asked. In an uncontrolled rush Julia told her everything and suddenly Ebbie was crying too. They grasped hands and struggled together with inarticulate grief, clumsily trying to offer each other comfort.

'It's what happened to you, isn't it?' Julia asked through her sobs.

'I'm not allowed to say,' Ebbie said, blowing her nose and trying to calm herself.

'You have to tell me. Did you have a baby?'

'Yes.' Ebbie nodded, her voice was almost inaudible.

'And they took it away.'

'Yes.' She nodded again, her response almost silent.

'Did you have a house like this?'

'Yes.'

'And now you're doing a menial job and living in one of their apartments.'

'Yes.'

'I want to get away.'

'You can't. You can't do it.'

'I'd rather go back to being an Outsider.'

'They'll find you. They'll find your friends and relations. They'll make their lives hell. You have to obey them or you and everyone suffers. You mustn't talk like this. It's too dangerous.'

'I don't care. I don't care. I need a friend so badly - and so do you.'

Ebbie took a pen and a piece of paper from the kitchen table drawer. She wrote,

The house is bugged. Our conversation will have been recorded already. Agree with what I tell you for both our sakes: we'll talk for real later, where it's safe. Julia stared at her dumbly. Ebbie said,

116

'I'll make us both a cup of tea. We'll soon feel better. It's not so bad, you know.'

'I suppose you're right.'

'You're very lucky really. And so am I. That outsider life, it's terrible. Don't let time blunt your memory of it. You wouldn't be able to bear it now.'

They drank tea sitting at the table and holding hands. A little later Ebbie wrote, *I'm sorry about this but I have my job to do and I'm not brave enough to go against them.*

Julia wrote,

I am!

After that Ebbie took the paper and burnt it and buried the ashes at the bottom of the garden. Julia went to bed and slept, oddly lulled by the faint hum of the vacuum cleaner.

36~

Giles Edward Fanshaw had been Master of an Oxford College and, as an undergraduate, Piers had known him. Affectionately referred to as GEF (pronounced Jeff) by friends and students alike, Fanshaw had always been an easy man to talk to. Now that he was the senior member of the Council of Electors it was natural for Piers to seek him out from time to time if only for old-times-sake. GEF and his wife had retired to a delightful villa on the lakeside just outside Geneva and Piers was invited there occasionally for an informal meal.

Struggling with the knotty question of Hugo Finch's election to the Parliament he accepted a dinner invitation gladly and, after the meal, when GEF's wife left them alone together, Piers began to unburden his mind.

'I have had such a life long hatred for this man that I'm forced to question my own judgement,' he said.

'On what is this hatred based?' The older man was watching Piers intently.

'Rivalries, dishonesty, petty things mostly. I hardly know him now. He may be one of the finest and most upright citizens in the British Isles.'

'But you have doubts.'

'I have to ask myself, do people really change?'

'You're asking if a dishonest man can become honest.'

'Yes.'

'I have rarely known it to happen, very rarely. The dishonest mind, like the criminal mind, seems to be ingrained in the personality. People may reform but it has to be a conscious decision. And then, under pressure they may revert. One is safest with men of integrity who do not have it in them to cheat.'

'I know you must be right. I simply wouldn't want to keep him out because of my own prejudice.'

'More dangerous to let him in because of it.'

'That's true.'

'If the council accepts him are you considering using your veto?'

'I don't want to have to speak against him to the Council, or even to you. I don't want it to come to that.'

'I don't suppose it will. This is neither the time nor the place for you to give me any concrete information on Finch but our investigations are already underway and they are extremely thorough. I'm not asking you for detailed evidence against him at this juncture, of course. That would amount to undue influence and we both know that is totally unacceptable in the present circumstances. I'm not open to your private influence any more than you would attempt to exert it.'

'That's not why I came here.'

'Nor is it why I invited you. You have told me that your mind is troubled concerning this man. I sympathise as a friend but as a member of the Council I shall pay no attention to what you have said unless you say it to the whole Council.'

37~

From the moment of the conversation in the kitchen with Ebbie Julia found a new strength. She had only one desire now and that was to get away. Ebbie, who had seemed so efficient and controlling, was suddenly anxious and terrified. Julia recognised that she had to think for both of them. She made her plans in secret and explained them to Ebbie outside in the park. She realised that Gareth, the man who had said he wanted to help her, had taken her outside to talk to her. Now she understood why. He had known that the house was bugged. He may even have known who had bugged it. Julia did not think she and Ebbie were important enough to merit government interest. There was some other organisation whose finances had been used to set them up and enslave them that had an interest in keeping them docile and obedient.

During one of their conversations in the park Ebbie had said that she had a mother living in a commune in Cornwall and had suggested that they go there. Julia had wanted time to think about that. On her own she would have no reason to go to Cornwall but with Ebbie the reason was clear and would probably be equally clear to whoever kept watch on them. Eventually she said,

'We can't go to Cornwall, Ebbie. It's so obvious that you'd want to go to your mother's place that it'd be like putting up a flag to show where we were going. They, whoever they are, would be there waiting for us.'

Ebbie seemed to comply with anything Julia said. It was like dealing with someone in a semi-catatonic state. Sometimes Julia wanted to shake her and shout at her to make her participate in the decision making.

'There's no bugs out here,' she said one day in exasperation. 'Tell me what you think. We're going to escape all this. You've been caught up in it longer than I have. Tell me what you think we ought to do.'

'I don't know,' said Ebbie.

'Well do you want to go or stay?'

'Go,' said Ebbie.

'Right then, we have to go somewhere. Where do you think we should go?'

'I don't know,' said Ebbie.

Julia was sometimes tempted to make a getaway at night on her own and let Ebbie come in the morning and find her gone. But she was afraid of what they might do to Ebbie and what Ebbie might say. If Ebbie warned them at once, as she might out of fear, Julia would have little hope of getting very far. If Ebbie were with her there would be no one to report on them until they were well away from London. What they needed was two backpacks and some Outsider clothes. For this purpose she began breaking down some of the items in her wardrobe, tearing them, dirtying them and trying to achieve that worn look of many years' grime that so many of the Outsiders had about them.

It was a long time before she showed them to Ebbie. It was good to see how impressed Ebbie was and how this one aspect of their plan seemed to give her hope.

'When we go,' she said, 'I'll leave the vacuum cleaner on and that will sound as if I'm still here working.'

'Not when the night comes and it's still on,' said Julia. 'What we need is a recording that can run for an hour or two every day. I could do that on a repeating track on the sound console, and we could talk a bit on it too. That might give us several days before they suspected anything.'

Ebbie provided the two backpacks and picnic food for several days. Julia did everything else. They put the Outsider clothes in a carrier bag to be discarded with their smart gear when they were well beyond the compound. The gate guards were the biggest problem. They knew their departure would be recorded on CCTV and entered in the log on the guard's computer. There was no getting round that. They came downstairs with their packs and the bag of clothes at ten-thirty in the morning. It was a good time to go shopping. They stood in the hall and were silent for a moment, looking at each other, wondering what they were taking on. At that moment there was a loud knocking on the door. A man's head with a characteristic hat on was visible through the glass.

'It's him,' said Ebbie in a whisper. 'It's the Agent man.'

'Put the bags in the cupboard,' whispered Julia. They hid the bags quickly and as silently as possible. When the knocking was repeated Julia ran forward and opened the door.

'Gareth!' she said with relief. Eden came in and shut the door behind him. He embraced Julia, to her surprise, and said

'You have to get away from here,' very quietly close to her ear. Julia led him to the cupboard and showed him the packs and the clothes in the bag.

'Good work,' he said. 'Come now. I have a car at the gate.'

'Ebbie too,' said Julia. Eden looked at the rather unprepossessing figure of Ebbie. 'We were just going shopping,' said Julia loudly. 'Ebbie and me, we need some new clothes. We were thinking of giving a party.'

'Come on,' he said.

'Wait!' said Julia and ran into the sitting room and switched on the recording.

'What was that,' Eden said as they walked towards the gates.

'Just a recording of us talking and the vacuum cleaner working. It's on a repeat track. It could keep them happy for days, whoever 'They' are.'

'You've been doing some serious planning,' said Eden.

'I've been angry enough to do anything, Gareth.'

'Good,' said Eden.

'The only trouble is, I don't know where on earth we're going.'

'I know where you're going,' he said.

38~

The large and beautiful circular room where the Council of Electors met had once been a library. It was reminiscent of the historic circular library that had long ago housed the book collection of the British Museum, before it became too large to be contained there. This library was also domed and, when first built in the seventeenth century, had been a church. It was not as high as the old British Museum Library but it offered some of the same comforts. Study alcoves were set into its circular structure and a range of galleries circled the walls giving access to the many reference books stored there. Naturally, in this day and age, computer terminals graced the tables in the alcoves and each member of the Council had a private computer, protected by his or her own password, giving access to the web and to the infinite pool of known information on any subject or person in the world.

Meetings were held at the great circular table under the dome and were conducted in complete secrecy. The First Minister alone had the right to be present when the Council discussed the potential election of members to the World Parliament. On this particular occasion Piers was not present and they were discussing a Taiwanese female candidate and a British male candidate. The British candidate was Hugo Finch.

The morning was given over to the sharing of information on the Taiwanese woman. She had the highest possible credentials and her sponsors in her own country were the Prime Minister and the head of the judiciary. She had served as a member of the Taiwanese Government for many years in the fields of Education and Science. Extensive research had produced no slur on her character and Piers Diamond had sought no opportunity to veto her application. After several hours' discussion it was decided that they should proceed to the interview stage in her case.

Hugo's case was tabled for after lunch. His sponsors were the Chief Whip of the British House of Commons and the Headmaster of the world famous Eton College, an example of superb education which had sustained its reputation as the best in the world for several centuries. The two members of the Council who had been given special responsibility for researching Hugo offered many favourable arguments but they were a little worried by the number of areas in his life about which nothing was known; they were also concerned that he seemed to be surprisingly unpopular in British Government circles. He was known to be a charming and erudite man and a successful lawyer. A joke was made at the expense of lawyers and their sometimes questionable methods of 'getting criminals off'. It was agreed that there was probably no lawyer living who had not made a few enemies. It was one of the hazards of the job. Despite the Council's varied concerns there was nothing serious reported against Hugo. His membership of the Elite Society came up and, since no one on the Council knew very much about the Elitists, it was decided that this should be looked into further. Giles Fanshaw mentioned obliquely that Piers Diamond had no liking for the ES and that he might wish to have a final say in this particular election for that reason. He also pointed out that the First Minister had been at school with the candidate and that there had been a clash of personalities then which the First Minister himself said might bias his judgement. The Council felt that there was nothing concrete at this juncture to prevent Hugo from being elected, but all agreed that they would like to defer final consideration of his application to a later date when more research had been done.

39~

The house on Wimbledon Common had looked dark and neglected when they arrived. It had smelt damp and rather sour. Its accustomed grime had consolidated with a kind of fungal quality while no one had been living there. On the way there, Eden had collected some boxes from the railway station. The boxes seemed to be full of papers. On the first night, as soon as they arrived at the house, the two girls had been so exhausted that they had simply fallen into the rather damp beds in their room and slept.

It had only taken Ebbie a matter of days to make the place clean and habitable. She was really quite obsessive about cleanliness. It had not been an over-zealous act at Julia's house, she really could not bear to see dust and grime. Now Julia and Eden had every reason to be grateful to her for this most basic instinct in her. The house had never been so beautifully kept during Eden and Prune's time there. She took on all the cooking and housekeeping. She did the shopping and she was happy to abide by the rules that Eden laid down. These rules were simple - no going out except once a week on differing days for essential items of food - no shopping except after dark and then only to the nearest mega-market where everything could be bought cheaply under one roof among faceless crowds of Outsiders - no speaking to anyone - no going out without a hood or cloth hat pulled well down. There were also rules about coming and going. The house must never be approached directly but circumnavigated once in each direction before either gate was unlocked. Eden had heavy blackout curtains at the windows and doors and neither the front nor the back door was to be opened for Ebbie without a recognisable knock from her, warning those inside to extinguish the lights first. Going near the windows was forbidden and if either of the girls forgot this Eden showed anger enough to ensure that they remembered in future.

It was a strange existence. Ebbie and Julia were happier in Eden's house than either of them had been with their Insider living conditions. Early on Eden showed them the shed not far from the house where his and Prunella's cycles were kept. One night he went out and made sure the tyres were pumped up. He seemed to think it important. He also made sure that they knew where the key to the shed was hidden, under a flagstone by the back gate. One day, over supper Julia asked about their need to know this.

'If we were discovered I ought to be able to engineer the chance for you to get away,' he said. 'No one could get a car in among these trees. On the bikes they'd never catch up with you.'

'Where would we go then?' Ebbie asked.

'To your mother in Cornwall, perhaps, or to one or other of the communes where you used to live.'

'You know about my mother?'

'Yes, I met her once. She'd be glad to see you, I know that. How long she could hide you I wouldn't like to say. Hiding people is a skilled occupation.'

'You seem to know a lot about it,' Julia said.

'I've had to learn,' he said calmly.

'We're lucky to know you,' Julia said.

'And I'm lucky to know you.'

'I wish we could repay you,' Ebbie said.

'So do I,' said Julia, 'but I'm afraid all we're doing here is putting you in danger.'

'I'm in much more danger than you could ever cause,' said Eden, 'but I'm used to it. I'd like to get you away from here for your own sakes before too long, but I may be going to need your help.'

Every day he was poring for long hours over a sheaf of papers at the desk in his own room. Neither of the girls would have presumed to ask what he was doing. Lately he had begun to work on an ancient note-book computer. Ebbie, bringing him tea or coffee at the times when she knew he liked a drink, saw that he was typing what appeared to be gibberish, or a foreign language she could not recognise. He worked intensely and was not to be interrupted. The girls whispered about what he might be doing and Ebbie reported on the strange words he was typing, but neither of them brought up the subject of his work in his presence.

The house was of a sturdy construction and its neglected appearance had not made it ramshackle. It was certainly not easy of access and no part of it was crumbling or likely to fall down. The front door was sturdy and opened into a hallway with a living-room on one side and a kitchen dining-room on the other. Outside the kitchen was a veranda with slim pillars and a sloping tile roof. The inside of this roof was lined with wood blocks in a pattern of squares. The wall of the kitchen was set back a few feet leaving a good space on the veranda for chairs and a table. In happier times and in summer weather people could have eaten out there. Eden and Prune had often done so. Now the table and chairs looked neglected and filthy and Ebbie was not allowed to go out and scrub them, much as she was longing to do so. The girls were surprised one morning to find that the table had been moved and the chairs stacked up at the far end of the veranda.

'Who moved the table and chairs?' asked Julia at breakfast.

'I did,' said Eden.

'When?'

'During the night?'

'Why?' said Ebbie.

'I had my reasons.'

'Won't someone notice?' asked Julia.

'I hope not. I had to take the risk.'

'Why?' asked both the girls.

'I think this is the moment to tell you something,' Eden said, and led the way upstairs into his room. He opened the wardrobe and pushed aside the clothes inside, revealing the back. He put his finger in a knot hole and the back slid aside revealing a door. Beyond the door was a narrow room, five feet by about eighteen. It stretched the length of the house above the veranda roof. The door had stout hasps for padlocks on the inside. In the corner at one end of the room a trapdoor with heavy bolts was set in the floor. It corresponded exactly to four squares of the wood-block decoration underneath. At the other end of the room was a low sink with a mains water tap. Two mattresses with some rolled blankets were leaning against the wall.

'A secret room,' said Julia.

'Yes,' said Eden. 'I hoped it wouldn't be necessary to show you this, but if the house were to be searched you and my work could be concealed here. Breaking in through this door would take a while. Plenty of time for you to drop down through the trapdoor onto the veranda table and make a getaway.'

'Would you be with us?' Ebbie was concerned.

'Not necessarily.'

'Is this the situation when you'd need our help?'

'If they come I shall need you to do one thing for me.'

'Go on.' Julia was anxious to know how dangerous things might get.

'The work I'm doing, whether or not it's finished, has to go to my brother. If the worst happens I shall want you to take the external chip, it's like a small pen, and get access to a computer, probably in a library, where you can get access to the web. When you open the document on the chip the first thing you'll see is the mail address to send it to. The document will be in code. No one will be able to read it except my brother. Don't worry about that. Just send it and get rid of the chip as quickly as you can. Drop it in a river, chuck it in an incinerator skip, anything you can think of to destroy it. Do you understand?'

'Yes. I understand completely. Is this coded document anything to do with the people who took my baby and Ebbie's?'

'It has everything to do with them, yes.'

'And will they be stopped? Will they be punished?'

'They certainly will.'

'When can we get started?' Julia was full of determination.

'Be patient. Evidence is needed against them. Without it they are going to gain even more power than they have now. I have the evidence. No one else in the world has it at the moment. Your experiences are part of it. I have to complete my work before the document can be sent. I hope to send it myself but if I'm prevented you must take it and do exactly as I've told you.'

'I'll do it,' said Julia. Ebbie looked frightened.

'You're much braver than me,' she said.

'I'm too angry to think about being brave,' Julia said.

'Good,' said Eden.

40~

It was only a matter of days before the knock came at the door. Eden's instinct had been right to confide in the girls when he did. They knew exactly what to do. The voice of the Agent echoed through the house at the second knock.

'Come out! I know you're here. Open the door or I shall blast the lock.'

'It's him. The Agent,' Julia whispered, white as a sheet.

'Come on,' said Eden, picking up a casual armful of food items from the table. 'Take what you can. Don't drop anything.'

They were inside the room and Eden had skipped back to his desk for his documents and the computer and then locked the wardrobe-back and the inner door's padlocks by the time they heard the Agent fire a shot, force the lock and kick the front door open. His footsteps were just audible as he patrolled the ground floor.

'He'll find the hot kettle,' Ebbie whispered.

'He won't find us, though,' said Eden.

'Can you be so sure?' Julia was still very white. 'What if he moves the wardrobe?'

'It's bracketed to the wall and cemented to the floor. It would take a bull-dozer to shift it.'

'Thank God for that.' Julia's hands were clammy and she was trembling. 'I'm afraid I'm going to be sick,' she said apologetically.

'Be our guest! There's the sink. Just do it quietly.' She did. She was as quiet as she could possibly be. When it was over she whispered,

'I'm sorry.' Eden pulled her down to sit by him and put his arm round her shoulders. 'I stink,' she said.

'It doesn't matter,' he said. 'We shall all have made a fair stink in here before we get out unless we're very lucky. We have to be tolerant of all that sort of thing.'

'I couldn't... I couldn't... you know...' said Ebbie.

'You'll get used to it,' said Eden.

They sat there, whispering, and breathing in the smell of Julia's vomit, and heard the Agent begin to mount the stairs. He went into the girls' room first. He was there a little longer than might have been expected. Then they heard him come into Eden's room. He moved about. They heard him shift one or two of the innocuous papers on the desk.

They held their breaths as he opened the wardrobe. He pushed the clothes aside, they heard the hangers clank together. Then there was a long silence. A scraping and clicking sound followed and then they heard the wardrobe door being closed. He moved away a few steps. They heard the bed creak. Then his voice, surprisingly distant considering the proximity, saying,

'Damian, can you hear me? - No one here. They were here. - Two at least. - I only just missed him. The kettle was hot. - I've bugged every room. - We'll know when to come back so, no problem. I don't need the two of you now. I'll be back at the car in five minutes. - Okay.' They heard him get up off the bed. They heard him go into the bathroom and relieve himself and pull the flush. They heard him go down the stairs and out of the front door, which he did not bother to close. They heard nothing more except their own breath released after being held for so long.

'Can we go out?' asked Ebbie. Julia put a hand over her mouth before she had finished the question.

'Shhh!' she whispered. 'There's a bug very close to us,'

'It's better not even to whisper,' Eden breathed. He indicated the paper and pen he had brought in with the computer. He put a small stack of clean paper on the floor between the girls. They would have to write anything they had to say.

For two days Eden sat on his mattress with his back to the door working feverishly at the computer. There was one electric socket in the room and at night, when the tiny single high window gave them no light, the blue glow of the computer screen lit up his features. The girls, sleeping intermittently and feeling as if they were caught in a nightmare, would wake to see his illuminated face tense above the little keyboard, and then turn over on their mattress and sleep again. No one made a sound. Julia was not sick again. They ate biscuits and cereal from the packet with their hands. They drank water from the tap. They moved as little as possible. Eden's abiding hope was to get his work finished before the Agent came back. He would be waiting for sounds of entry to the house. While there was no sound he would surely stay away. On the third day, when Eden's work was almost finished, Ebbie sneezed. They all froze. Eden grabbed the pen and paper,

130

'That's it! Be ready.'

Typing frantically, he continued his work. His face poured sweat. The girls could do nothing. Julia was alert and ready to move the moment he said go. Ebbie was restless and deeply upset by the smelly hole the room had become. She wanted nothing but to get out. Time gripped and held them. Eden's fingers stumbled, becoming stiff with intensity and exhaustion. The end was in sight. He curtailed the last paragraphs to the barest minimum. He saved the work and yanked the short, pen-shaped chip out of its socket in the computer, thrust a cap on it and put it into Julia's hand.

'Do exactly as I told you.' His whisper was urgent but almost silent.

'Yes,' she nodded and he leapt to the corner, lifted the girls' mattress, pulled back the bolts on the trapdoor and lifted the flap. The table was visible about five feet below.

'Let yourself hang through on your elbows and then drop,' he whispered. Julia positioned herself and hesitated for a moment. As she did so they all heard the sound of voices below. Not just one voice this time, three men at least.

'Wait!' Eden hardly articulated the word but it went through Julia like an electric current. Eden was at the door, unfastening the padlocks.

'What are you doing?'

'Going out. You have to get away while I keep them occupied.'

'No.' Julia was almost distraught.

'Do as I told you. Go for the bikes. When you hear me laugh go out through the trapdoor. It will be safe only when they're all in my room. They won't be able to see you from there. Be ready. When I laugh, go!'

He didn't say goodbye or good luck and nor did they. He was out through the wardrobe in seconds. They heard its back close. Ebbie, unbidden, replaced the padlocks. They heard the bed creak. Eden was lying down to greet them as if they had woken him, Julia supposed. The girls heard the shout of, 'Here he is.' They heard the feet pounding on the stairs. They heard Eden say,

'Well, well, gentlemen, this is a surprise. Was it you who broke my front door lock a few days ago?'

They heard the Agent's voice,

'Cut the crap.' They heard Eden laugh.

Julia let herself down on her elbows and then dropped. The table was sturdy. Ebbie looked down through the hole.

'I can't,' she whispered.

'Yes, you can,' said Julia, 'and if you can't I'm going.' Ebbie slithered her legs over the edge and Julia got hold of them. 'Good,' she whispered, 'that's it.' She helped Ebbie down and they got off the table as quietly as they could. Julia unlocked the back gate and overturned the paving stone beside it. The shed key was there. They ran then. The paths were trodden earth and their feet made hardly any sound. The lock on the shed was well oiled, so were the bikes. Their mechanisms purred as they were wheeled out. It was a reassuring sound. The house looked dead, blank, empty. They mounted the bikes and fled along the path among the trees in the direction of Wimbledon Library.

Unwashed and stinking, Julia went up to the library desk and pre-paid for a computer terminal with mailability. The chip slid into the slot in the side and the computer offered her the choice of copying, editing or mailing the data. She chose mailing and waited for the window to come up. It showed. She opened the document, copied and pasted it complete and then looked at the mail address at the top. It read, 'PiersDiamond@W.G.Geneva'. Julia could not believe her eyes. He had said the document must be mailed to his brother. His brother was the First Minister of the World Parliament. They had just spent days and nights shut in a hell-hole with the brother of Piers Diamond. That was who had rescued her. She sat staring at the gobbledygook document that stretched out of sight beyond the bottom of the screen. She typed the address in the box, put the pointer on 'send' and clicked. The text turned green, as it always did on a successful mailing. She selected it all again and deleted it. She went to the 'sent items' window and deleted it there. She selected the whole document on the chip and pressed 'delete'. A message came up on the screen, 'Access denied.' She tried again. The same thing happened. The chip was permanent and not re-writable. She took out the chip and put the cap on it. She really had to lose it, and soon. The woman at the desk called out to her as she passed,
'I didn't get you to fill in a form. I hope you didn't delete your mail?'
'Yes,' said Julia, 'I'm afraid I did.'
'But you left it in the 'sent box?'
'No.'
'Will you fill in this form, please. We have to keep a record of all mail sent from public libraries. I'd have thought you knew that, you seem very au fait with computers.'
'I forgot,' said Julia. Outside she saw Ebbie holding the bikes. 'I must go.'

'Not without filling in the form,' said the woman sternly.

'Give it to me,' said Julia, 'It was just a greeting on behalf of a friend to his brother.'

'Right, I'll do it for you. What was the brother's name?'

'Err .. Peter Ruby,' said Julia.

'We shall be able to check, you know. A greeting to the brother of a friend, you said.' She was writing. 'What was the name of the friend?'

'Err .. it was . . . it's John, John Gareth.'

'Anything untoward and we shall trace you, very easily.'

'It's all fine,' said Julia. 'You won't need to waste time tracing me.'

'Sign here,' said the librarian, 'and print your name underneath.' Julia signed with a squiggle and a flourish and then printed 'Jane Derby'. She did not seem to be able to invent names without linking them in some way to recent experiences. It was a criminal offence to give a false name, she knew that perfectly well, but it seemed less of a risk than giving her own name. She ran with the chip in her pocket to where Ebbie was waiting and they set off at speed.

'We have to get to the river,' said Julia.

'Is it near?' Ebbie had no idea of the geography of outer London.

'If we turn and go back to Wandsworth we'll come to it easily,'

'Can't we go on towards the west country? It doesn't seem very safe to go back towards London.'

'I take your point but if we're caught and I have the chip on me we're done for.'

'I don't really see why. Wasn't it all in code?'

'Yes.'

'Who did you have to mail it to?'

'Never mind.'

'Someone we know?'

'No, of course not.'

'What was the mail address?'

'I can't remember. It was complicated.'

'Did you blank the chip?'

'Delete the contents, you mean?'

'Yes.'

'I couldn't. It was 'access denied'.'

'We had better lose it, then.'

'That's what Gareth said.'

'Do you think he's all right?'

'I don't know, Ebbie. I'm scared for him.'

They didn't go back, they went on, and near Maidenhead they made a slight detour and Julia threw the chip into the Thames. Then they went on to Reading and left the bikes in the station yard and got on the next train to Bodmin. It was wonderful to sit down and be able to relax. They had sandwiches and coffee on the train. No one came to sit near them because they stank.

41 ~

The Agent travelled to Geneva on the overnight flight. He was inside the World Government building before most of the employees had arrived for work. He had impressive credentials that included a letter of introduction to the First Minister signed by his brother. He was asked to wait. Naturally the First Minister was still at his residence. He would be in his office by ten and would possibly be able to see the Agent soon after eleven. The Agent was given a place to sit and a cup of coffee. He drank the coffee and then began to wander about. He very soon found the outer office of the First Minister's department and greeted the first secretary to arrive in a warm and charming manner. It was not long before he had persuaded her to let him use a computer terminal in the office to collect important mail of his own from the web. She took a little persuading but she had her work to do and there were certainly free terminals at this hour of the day. She powered up one of them for him and went back to her own.

It took the Agent only a matter of minutes to hack into the incoming mail at the First Minister's address. He found the coded message sent by Julia from the Wimbledon Library and deleted it. He then went into 'deleted mail' and deleted it permanently. Before doing this he had printed out one copy. This he folded small, since it comprised only one sheet of paper, and placed it in the zip compartment of his wallet. There would be time later to present it to Eden and find out if he was able to crack the code. It was vital to find out how much Eden had actually discovered. In the meantime, he was certain of protecting Hugo Finch's name and relieving the World Government of the problem of Jason Marn.

42~

The Elitists Society owned a beautifully preserved, early Georgian mansion in the English countryside. Its extensive parklands, including a well-concealed factory farm, were surrounded by the most up-to-date barrier-fence and the gates were heavily guarded. Here Eden was taken and incarcerated in a room in the basement. It was an extraordinarily glamorous prison. The floor was made of green marble tiles as shiny as glass. Three of the walls were black marble and the remaining one was faced with stainless steel which gave the effect of a mirror. It was by no means a small room. In two of the corners were gratings in the floor with shower fitments above. Eden was soon to discover that these sprayed fierce jets of water twice a day for about three minutes. He was also to discover that the floor was temperature controlled. When he arrived it was quite warm. It could, however be made extremely cold or extremely hot at the whim or intention of some operator elsewhere. At first sight it seemed there was no bed but Eden soon found the six foot by three-foot shelf which folded into the wall at one of the free corners. This provided a very comfortable bed with a thick mattress, warm bedding and several pillows, the bed linen was a tasteful wine colour which made the bed look cosy unless a morbid imagination suggested that it was also the colour of blood. When it was locked up against the wall Eden found that the bed could not always be opened. It could in fact be closed and retained in the locked position according to the will of his captors. A form of deprivation designed to create the maximum effect, he realised. There was nothing else in the room except a tap above one of the gratings and a plastic drinking glass on a small shelf that was close to the bed-head when the bed was open. Illumination was by several small spotlights sunk in the ceiling. Eden was not easily frightened but this room, with its cold, rather theatrical appearance, made him feel apprehensive. He was tired when he got there. Unable to make either of the showers work he had a brief wash under the tap, drank some water and got into bed. He slept for hours. When he woke again most of the ceiling lights were out which made him assume that it was night. Hazily he realised that they could make him think night was day or day was night by manipulating the lights in a windowless room. He was too exhausted to contemplate the complexities of his situation then and there. He went back to sleep and woke to find the lights on and a guard unlocking the door to bring him some breakfast. It was a very nice breakfast, real coffee and plenty of warm rolls with butter and a choice of preserves in little jars. The kind of breakfast still called 'continental' on the menus of old fashioned English hotels. He ate hungrily. During his meal both the showers gushed suddenly in their corners. He was too late to get more than a brief dousing but the water was warm and he felt quite hopeful as, dripping and naked he stood by his bed finishing his breakfast. If he timed it right he could get a decent shower next time. He wondered if they would let him have towels and perhaps some books. When he asked they allowed both. The books were not what he would have wished but at least he had some footling romances and adventure stories to read. After some hours he discovered a panel in the wall that concealed a television. It seemed to be connected to only one channel and that gave a perpetual stream of news. Eden didn't mind that. He was in fact delighted. He could switch it on or off as he wished. He had no means of knowing whether the news was live or recorded. He suspected it was recorded as one or two of the stories seemed to become rather repetitive, but then that was often the case with news programmes and he had not had access to the current news for some days so it was impossible for him to judge. He watched political items avidly for information about Piers but there was none. He kept the television on most of the time once he had found it. Otherwise he slept a lot at first. He was surprisingly well fed. He assumed he was a hostage. This would be a good thing. It would mean his life was not in immediate danger. He relaxed and waited for developments.

43~

The Agent knew better than to push his luck. He left the World Government building with the coded document in his wallet and went to a nearby hotel where he booked a room for one night, ordered a large breakfast to be served in his room and began making a series of phone calls. The first of these was to purchase a rowing boat that was to be delivered to him at a landing stage in a deserted section of the lake shore. The last was to room service, instructing them to order a car to take him to the airport early the next morning. In between he spoke to Hugo and then to Partridge. His penultimate call was to David . . . He did not identify himself when he heard David's voice, he simply stated his case.

'We have the First Minister's brother. You have Jason Marn on your hands. I'd like to think we could do a deal.' David knew that Piers was in a serious dilemma over the question of Jason Marn. His conscience would not allow him to give the nod to the boy's 'disappearance' and yet they both knew that David could not possibly sanction letting the boy go. The Agent waited for his words to sink in for a moment or two before saying, 'Would you like us to meet?'

'Where?' David was highly suspicious.

'A quiet place. No one need ever know. I have only one condition.'

'Go on.'

'You bring the boy. No one else.'

David hesitated. 'Did you hear me?'

'Yes,' said David. 'I heard you. I need to think. Can you ring back?'

'Fifteen minutes,' said the Agent. The line went dead. David put his phone in his pocket and went out of the building. He walked along the lake path out of hearing of any of the adjoining buildings. He sat on a seat looking at the lake. He had not spoken to Piers. He had no intention of speaking to Piers. He knew what Piers would say. David was desperate for a deal that would get them off the hook. This man was clever. Perhaps he had such a deal in mind. The phone buzzed. David activated it and said,

'Hello.'

'Have you thought?'

'Yes. Why do you want me to bring the boy?'

'If we do a deal he's there and ready. If we don't it will be simple enough for you to take him back again.'

'Yes, I see that. And in exchange?'

'I told you, we have Piers' brother.'

'Are you bringing him too?'

'David, we're not talking about a rent-boy now. Eden Diamond is a very clever espionage specialist. He lives as an Outsider and has everyone fooled. He could destroy you, he could destroy me. He has trumped up information on Hugo Finch, for instance, that could stop his election to the World Parliament if it gets to Piers. That would be very bad for the British representation on the world stage.'

'Very bad for you and the people who're paying you, you mean.'

'Who do you think is paying me, David?'

'The Elitist Society I imagine, or Hugo Finch himself.'

'Hugo couldn't afford me, David, not at the level of this transaction.'

'So, what are you offering me in exchange for Jason?'

'Eden's release, perhaps, without our having to make any approach to Piers?'

'What do you think Piers is going to do if you approach him?'

'Put his word in for Hugo with the Electors, perhaps. After all his brother's life must mean something to him.'

'You don't know Piers.'

'And Piers doesn't know me. But I have a wonderful letter of introduction to him, signed by his brother, though written by me of course. It's in my pocket as we speak.'

'I'll meet you.'

'Not without the boy.'

'Very well. I'll bring the boy.'

'Good. One-fifteen a.m. at the landing stage at the far end of the Krugen's property. They're away in the States. There's only a rather deaf caretaker in residence. After midnight they never have the beach patrolled. We shall have complete privacy. They can't afford expensive security. Watch your step on the landing stage. The planks are starting to rot.'

Just after one a.m. David brought Jason to the landing stage. The Agent was there before them. As they approached along the lakeside path they could see him standing on the end of the jetty, silhouetted against the moon-reflecting lake. It was a cold but beautiful night. They made their way along the rotting planks. A small rowing boat was moored at the foot of the slimy steps that led down into the water. David's gun was in Jason's ribs and he had hold of Jason's arm. It had been a longish walk. They had hardly spoken. Now the Agent said,

'Hello, Jason.'

'So it's you,' said Jason. 'What now?'

'I've come to take you away from these people.' The Agent was smiling confidently in the dimness. It would have been darker had it not been for the lake and the moon.

'Not so fast,' said David. 'I want some reassurances, some proof of what we discussed.'

'Here's the letter.' Both men had guns. Jason would have had no chance of making a dash for it. The letter changed hands. David used his pen-torch.

'And this is the original.'

'Oh, yes, I swear to you.'

'I wasn't questioning that. I can see it's the original. So what's the deal?'

The Agent took charge very suddenly.

'Jason, get in the boat.' He had his gun to Jason's head as the boy descended the steps. He didn't follow him. He stood on the jetty beside David. When Jason was in the boat he fired. The first and second bullets went through the boy's skull. The subsequent bullet went into his chest and the rest punctured the bottom of the boat. It began slowly to fill with water which grew dark with the stain of blood. 'That's one of your problem's solved,' said the Agent. He went down a few steps, untied the boat and pushed it away from the landing stage with one of its oars. He threw his gun into the boat and dropped the oar in the water. He had not taken his gloves off. 'The lake is very deep here. No one will find him, unless, of course, you choose to tell them.' He came back onto the jetty, took out his second gun, checked it and put it away again. 'Shall we go back on land, or would you like to watch it sink? Suicide is always so sad, don't you think - if anyone could be persuaded that's what it was.' They made their way back along the landing stage in silence and began to walk along the tree-lined path. 'Now, perhaps we can discuss the genuine deal,' the Agent said.

'You think I'm going to thank you for this?'

'No, but I think you're probably very grateful nevertheless. But we have more important things to consider.'

'Go on.'

'Eden Diamond has collected a considerable amount of black propaganda against Hugo Finch.'

'So? What do you want me to do?'

'Ignore it. Discredit it. At best, suppress it. At all events keep it away from Piers, as I am trying to do.'

'If the press get hold of it neither you nor I will be able to stop them.'

'The press mustn't get hold of it.'

'How could I control that, even if I wanted to? - which I don't. I have no time for the Elitists or for detestable men like Hugo Finch.'

'If the press get hold of anything bad about Finch they will undoubtedly also hear about Jason's death,' said the Agent quietly. 'After all, you were there and armed, with a gun coincidentally identical to the one that's in the boat. I was just a witness. I have no gun of that make and never have had. You were doing Piers' work. I was trying to save the boy. A rent boy with whom Piers had a relationship that you and he were trying to cover up. 'Who touches pitch will be defiled', remember.'

'Will you let Eden go?'

'Of course. When Hugo's election is secure.'

'And what if Piers himself vetoes it?'

'Then he may not see his brother alive again. Is that what you want for him? I think it's quite simple, don't you? Quite clear?'

'I have nothing more to say. I can't possibly agree to co-operate.'

'You don't have to agree. Your co-operation is taken for granted. I'll leave you here. My hotel is this way. I'd love to go on talking but I have a very early flight booked in the morning so I'll say good night.'

'Don't take too much for granted,' David said.

'Oh, no. I only ever bet on certainties.' The Agent walked away without looking back and was soon lost in the lights and shadows of the street of sophisticated hotels and cafes.

44~

The second printer in the First Minister's outer office was out of paper. The secretary to his PA put a sheaf of paper in the tray and turned the printer on. It went into action at once, producing a single paragraph headed 'page 2 of 2' addressed as mail to PiersDiamond@W.G.Geneva. The paragraph was in complete gibberish but secretaries at Geneva were used to codes. The secretary handed it to the PA who took it through to Piers' office and put it on his desk. When Piers came in he looked at it, looked at it again and put it aside. Some code or language that was unfamiliar to him was not for the moment. He worked at paperwork and diplomatic interviews all the morning. He was due to have lunch with the German Chancellor but there was a last minute cancellation because the Chancellor had a serious bout of flu and had to be careful of a weak chest and could not risk the flight. Unexpectedly free for once, Piers took the incomprehensible mail across to his residence and pondered over it while he ate a rather lavish diplomatic meal alone. The last word aroused a faint memory. It was ATAO. A signature? A company name? Those letters had once had some connection for him. He sipped a frugal glass of German wine, a vintage that had been chosen as a compliment to the Chancellor and to make him feel at home. Eden's face came into focus in his mind's eye. It had something to do with Eden. Of course, Eden was ATAO - and Piers was FHAA3N. This had been their code. Eden had invented it as a teenager and had always enjoyed using it more than Piers did. They had taken their favourite composers, Mahler and Mozart and constructed a twenty-six letter sequence from their names:

GUSTAVMAHLERWOLFGANGMOZART. Any letter appearing more than once in the sequence was simply identified by a number following it to show which A, of which there were four, or M or O, of which there were two, was intended. Piers at Oxford had found it tedious when Eden had written to him in code. He had often set Eden's letters aside to be deciphered later and sometimes never got round to it. Now he brought pencil and paper to his beautifully decorated lunch table and wrote out the sequence of letters at the top of a sheet. Slowly the last paragraph of Eden's desperate communication became clear.

. . .have evidence against Hugo Finch. Papers incriminating HF and all the ES are in the safe of Ian Derbyshire. He lives in Hampstead compound nr Swiss Gate. I have copies can't get them to you. Go for originals. Act with care. Prune sometimes stays with Derbyshires. ES are racists and cannibals. I have witnesses, two girls I have rescued. I am in hiding and in danger of capture by ES but I hope to get the girls away. I shall try to reach Una if poss. Eden.

Piers read and reread the paragraph. As evidence it counted for nothing. It read like a boys' comic-strip adventure. Was Eden exaggerating? He certainly seemed to have got in over his head and was in serious danger. He now knew he must instigate an investigation of the ES officials without seeming to do so. If what Eden said was even half true Hugo and the ES were finished.

45~

Prune continued to be content to stay with the Derbyshires. She got on well with the children and Valerie showed more sympathy for her as time went on. She liked the idea of befriending Piers Diamond's strange little sister and occasionally allowed herself to boast about the contact to members of her social circle. She did not actually say that she and her family knew Piers Diamond, or even that she had met him, but she liked the fact that people assumed this to be the case and sometimes failed to contradict the assumption. Ian, on the other hand, was increasingly uncomfortable at having Piers Diamond's half-sister in the house. He was made doubly uncomfortable by her retardedness and her looks. He hated abnormality. He was in deep agreement with the declared policy of the British Government to abort Down's Syndrome foetuses. He wanted to stop Prune coming to the house and when Valerie confided to him that she would like to adopt Prune he was shocked and disgusted.

'What are you thinking of?' he said, 'Do you want to turn our family into a freak-show?' Valerie was repelled by his response. She knew that he was busy with work and the ES treasurership and that being over-stretched always made him edgy but she refused to allow him to get away with voicing such an attitude. They quarrelled seriously over the subject and, after Ian said he wanted Prune out of the house by the next day and that it was to be made clear that she could not stay overnight again, Valerie stated that she intended to tell Prune that this was her home for as much time as she wanted to stay, and always would be. From the little spare room, which the family had made her own, Prune heard this conversation once voices were raised. Lucy came in, having heard it too, and sat on Prune's bed and began to tell silly jokes, trying to make her laugh and to drown out her parents' voices. However, jokes or no jokes, when Ian said what he did about the family being turned into a freak-show, Prune began to cry. Lucy hugged her and mopped her up in a very motherly fashion but what had been heard could not be unheard and from that moment Prune felt unsafe in the house and vindictive towards Ian.

She was not a free agent and it was difficult for Prune to make decisions. She had always been able to depend on Eden. Now he seemed to have disappeared. She had tried to phone him and she had sent him numerous texts but there was no response. She would already have become very scared except that Valerie and the children had, up to now, always made her feel safe. She knew that Eden would come back for her in the end, of course, and that she must wait, as always, until he told her what to do. After overhearing the terrible conversation, she began to think of getting away. The only person she could think of going to was Una and she did not really know where Una lived. She didn't have a phone number for Una because Una didn't hold with modern gadgetry. Una had a land-line but Prune didn't know the number. The only thing she could remember was High Wycombe, but she had no idea if that was the name of Una's house or if it was the nearest place to where Una lived. She decided not to ask any of the Derbyshires for help. Wanting to leave them was her secret and she didn't intend to have to fight them. If she decided to go, she was going, and no one was going to stop her.

There was no more shouting from Ian and Valerie's room but, as she waited to go to sleep for her remaining nights in the house, Prune thought about her plan to run away to Una. She became more and more convinced that High Wycombe was the place and, after a day or two, when Ben was working on his Geography project, she looked in his atlas and saw where High Wycombe was. It looked very close to London. It was definitely on the west side. She knew the train to Reading went from Paddington. She could see Reading very near High Wycombe. It looked as if it must be about half an hour's walk. It never occurred to her that the map might be on rather a small scale, causing the place names to look disproportionately big and close to each other. That night she went up to bed early. She didn't get undressed but put all her belongings in her backpack. Then she sat on the bed and waited to hear the family come up to their rooms. Lucy looked in to see if she was all right and was surprised to see her sitting on her bed fully dressed,

'What are you doing, Prunie?' she said. 'I thought you were tired.'

'I wanted to think,' said Prune importantly.

'Okay. Well, get into bed now, won't you?'

'Yes,' said Prune. 'I shall go to bed eventually.'

'I think you should go right now,' said Lucy.

'Okay,' said Prune and Lucy went away.

She was still sitting on the bed when she heard the house phone ring. She heard Ian answering it in the hall. It was obvious that the grandmother was worse. It was obvious that they had to go to the hospital. Valerie came into Prune's room a little while later.

'Prune, darling,' she said, 'Grandma is suddenly worse and we have to go to the hospital. I don't know what to do about you. Lucy could stay with you but she wants so much to see her Grandma this time.'

'Yes,' said Prune, with her customary directness. 'She might be going to die.'

'We hope not, dear,' said Valerie, 'but I have to admit it is possible.'

'You can leave me here,' said Prune. 'If anything goes wrong I'll just call the gate guard. I'm not stupid, you know and I'm not a freak. I can look after myself until you get back.'

'Of course you're not a freak,' Valerie said, and Prune was gratified to see that she was looking rather worried by the phrase.

'Off you go,' said Prune. 'If I don't like it here alone I'll get my brother to come and fetch me.'

'I don't think the First Minister is in this country at the moment.'

'No,' said Prune, 'I don't mean Piers, I mean my other brother.'

'I didn't know you had another brother. I thought you lived with your godmother at a compound near, where was it, High Wycombe.'

'It's not a compound,' said Prune and then bit her lip, 'Well, it sort of is.'

'Of course it is,' said Valerie, 'Only those country compounds don't have to be so strictly guarded as the London ones.'

'No,' said Prune. 'Anyway, I could go there if I got scared here.'

'You don't need to get scared, do you?'

'No,' said Prune.

'I'm sure we'll be back by breakfast time, or Ian will at least because he has work to do in the morning.'

'Is Grandma his mother?' Prune asked.

'No,' said Valerie, 'Grandma is my mother.'

'I hope she doesn't die then,' said Prune.

They left her alone and when the sound of the car had died away Prune took her back-pack and went downstairs. She went into Ian's study and looked at his horrible desk and his horrible chair. She took a dagger shaped paper knife and wondered if it would be a good idea to pay him out for his beastliness by sticking it through his chair. She decided against this. Then she had the most marvellous idea. She pulled his chair over to the safe, climbed up and swung the Picasso print out of the way. She knew the date and year of Lucy's birthday. In a short time she had the safe open. There were quite a lot of papers inside and a cash box. She took them out and placed them carefully on the desk. She opened the cash box and found a stack of bank notes inside. She took some of them, not all, she didn't want to be greedy and she didn't want to punish Ian more than he deserved. She put the little stack of notes into the small side pouch of her back-pack.

Then she stuffed all the papers into the main compartment of the pack. It meant squashing her pyjamas and her washing things very tight but she managed to get everything in. She could only partly zip the bag up but that was no problem, nothing was going to fall out when she had it upright on her back. She climbed back onto the chair and closed the safe. Then she got down and put the chair back where it belonged. Eden would be so pleased with her. He would have all the papers now, not just copies of a few. The thought of Eden reminded her that she had seen him do something particular when he had been in a place where he should not have been. He wiped everything clean of 'prints' if he wasn't wearing gloves. Prune was not sure what 'prints' were exactly but she knew it had to do with touching things. She went out into the hall where a fine silk scarf of Valerie's was hanging over the back of a chair. She took it back into the study, put the chair back under the safe, climbed up and wiped everything she had touched. Then she got down, replaced the chair and wiped it carefully. Picked up her pack and went back to the hall, wiping the door-handles of the study door as she went. She put the scarf back where she had found it and went out of the front door. It shut behind her with a firm click and she knew she could not get in again. It occurred to her that the Julia lady might help her if asked but Julia's house looked dark and deserted. Prune went to the gate and smiled at the guard who was a man she knew well.

'The Derbyshire's grandmother may be dying,' she said, 'They had to leave me to get packed and now I'm going to stay with my godmother.'

'Righty ho,' said the man, 'Find your way all right, can you?'

'Oh, yes,' said Prune sounding much more certain than she felt. 'I'm going to get a train from Paddington.'

'You'll need to get a move on. The last train goes within the hour. Shall I get you a taxi?'

'Yes, please,' said Prune. She could well afford a taxi.

At Reading she saw an extraordinary sight. Her bicycle and Eden's were chained up in the station yard. She searched around the station for a while, expecting to find Eden. He was clever enough to be there to meet her, even though she hadn't been able to ring him. After a while she gave up the search and fished in her bag and found the spare key to the bike lock that Eden had insisted she keep there. She unlocked her bike chain and, after another brief look round, set off on the road signposted to High Wycombe. Eden must have left the bike there for her. He was somewhere about. Una would be sure to know. She seemed to be lost several times but the bike was in good working order and eventually she began to recognise features of the countryside. When she was within half a mile of Una's gate she knew exactly where she was. She turned into the driveway and got off the bike, the better to negotiate the potholes in the dark. She didn't go directly to the house but left her bike by a tree and went to the old chest sunk in the earth where Una kept her most precious tools. She knew exactly where to find the padlock key. She opened the chest and put all the papers carefully inside. She also put in some of the bank notes and placed a large stone on top of them to keep them together. After that she locked the chest again and proceeded to the house. When Una, amazed, answered her knock, brought her in and heated some soup for her, Prune told her nothing about the papers. She told her all about the Derbyshires though, and the horrible conversation she had overheard.

'Never mind,' said Una. 'You stay here now. You're safe here.'

'Eden's coming too,' said Prune. 'He'll be here soon. His bike's at the station.'

46~

If one thing was clear from the coded mail sheet, of which Piers had only part, it was that the evidence against Hugo and the Elitists was to be found in the safe at Ian Derbyshire's family home in the Hampstead and Highgate compound. This being the case Piers contacted MI5 and requested a search of the property.

Ian and the family got back from visiting Grandma in the early hours of the morning. Prune was nowhere to be seen, but that was the least of their worries and Lucy remembered that she had said she might go to her Godmother's. By the time this was mentioned a great deal had happened. Ian had noticed the long black vehicle parked discreetly inside the gates. He knew what it meant and his heart sank. If he was about to be arrested his main object was to keep Valerie and the children from knowing any of the details. He was vulnerable in two areas; his notebook computer and the safe. The safe was fortunately well concealed behind the Picasso print and he dared to hope it would not be discovered. The laptop was in its case in the boot of the car. He contemplated leaving it there. He knew it was pointless. He made a snap decision and hurried into the house. Putting down some random items of luggage in the hall he went into his study and called Lucy to follow him.

'Shut the door,' he said abruptly.

'What have I done now?' she asked petulantly.

'Nothing,' he said, 'I need your help.'

'What?'

'I need you to be very grown-up, Lucy, and say noting to your mother or Ben about this.' He was unlocking the French-windows that went into the back garden.'

'About what?' said Lucy suspiciously.

'I want you to go to the car and get the small black case with my laptop in it. Do it quickly and come back here. Don't stop, don't speak to anyone and if anyone speaks to you pretend you didn't hear them. Be quick!'

'Why?'

'Lucy, for once just do as I ask you and don't argue.' Lucy dropped the backpack that was over her shoulder onto the floor and went sullenly out of the room, stomping with her feet in a rather childish manner.

'Grow up, Lucy,' her father shouted after her.

'Grow up yourself,' she shouted back.

In about a minute and a half, which seemed an eternity to Ian, Lucy reappeared with the laptop in its case.

'There you are,' she said, 'Mission accomplished.'

'Not quite,' her father said.

'Urrhh! What now?'

'Lucy, I want you to do this quickly and ask no questions.'

'Wha-at?' Lucy was bored with this game of errands for Daddy.

'Take the laptop down the garden. Put it under the tarpaulins that are folded up at the back of the shed. Then come straight back in here and go on helping your mother to clear the car.'

'Do what?

'You heard me. Go down to the shed with this and hide it, for Christ's sake.'

'Okay. Keep your pants on.'

'Lucy!'

'Sorry. I'm going. Look! I'm going.' She disappeared and was back before he dared hope for it.

'Now get on with clearing the car,' he said.

'What about you? Leaving it to the women and children are you?'

'There's not that much, Lucy. We only went for one night.'

'At least Grandma's getting better.'

'Yes. That's something to be thankful for.'

She picked up her backpack and went to the door.

'Lucy,' he said, and when she looked back, 'thank you.'

'Real!' she said, 'a thank-you from my Dad. That must be a first.'

The car was already cleared and as Lucy went into the hall she saw her mother talking to two men in suits who were standing on the doorstep.

'We do have a search warrant,' one of them was saying. Lucy stopped in her tracks and held her breath. Something was seriously wrong and she hadn't realised it. The men were shown into her father's study and she and her mother and Ben hovered at the door. One of the men explained to Ian that they had a search warrant and that they needed to look in his safe.

'I believe it's behind here,' the man said pointing to the Picasso.

'Who are you?' Ian said confrontationally. 'We've just spent the night at the bedside of my mother-in-law who is in hospital in a critical condition and we come back to this. Have you got some form of identification?' It was a sad ploy, an ineffectual delaying tactic. The two men produced their MI5 identification and Ian's heart sank utterly. There was nothing for him to do then but open the safe. Futile pretences such as not remembering the combination would simply have made him look more foolish. He was done for. The ES was done for. Hugo was done for. It was a sorry situation. He swung the Picasso back and turned the dial to the six points required to release the lock. He wondered if the men would be discreet in what they said in front of his family. He wondered if it would be immediate arrest. If they took the papers away to study them, perhaps he could make it to the airport and get on a plane to - somewhere - anywhere. He pulled the door of the safe open. There was nothing inside but his cash box and his velvet bag of uncut gems. He turned to the men. I mustn't crow, he told himself, holding back on his astounding relief. I must seem to have expected to see this exactly as it is. He took the cash box and the gems and put them on his desk. One of the men opened the cash box. The other tipped the gems out onto the desk. Their faces showed a degree of surprise and disappointment. They looked at each other.

'Do you have a laptop?' one of them said.

'I do,' said Ian, trying to keep the nervous jubilation out of his voice, 'but it's gone to be repaired.'

'Where would that be, then?' the other man asked. They were not going to give up all that easily.

'I forget the man's name,' said Ian. 'He does all our IT repairs and so forth. He comes to the house periodically. He's called Dick, I seem to remember.

'Dick Ridgeway,' said Lucy suddenly, moving from the doorway into the room.

'Is it, darling?' said Ian, 'I'm sure you're right.'

'Have you got a receipt or any paperwork relating to the transaction. You won't have let him take your laptop away without some form of security,' said one of the men.

'Especially when you hardly know his name,' said the other.

'I didn't bother with any of that,' said Ian, laughing at his own carelessness. 'I'm obviously not as suspicious as you gentlemen.'

'I could get him on the phone,' said Lucy. 'I know his number.'

'Would you do that, Miss?' the first man said. Ian was white. Lucy keyed in a number and held out her phone to the officer.

'Be my guest,' she said. The man took the phone and held it to his ear for a few moments. A voice at the other end was saying, 'You have reached the voice mail of Richard Ridgeway. Please leave a message and I'll get back to you.' The man nodded and put the phone back in Lucy's hand. They looked at each other again and, seeming to agree silently that the time had come to leave, they went towards the door.

'Sorry to have bothered you, sir,' said the one who seemed to be the senior of the two.

'That's all right,' said Ian, 'I'm just a bit bemused, that's all.'

'We're simply acting on instructions,' said the senior officer. 'I hope we won't have to trouble you again.'

'So do I,' said Ian, checking himself from sounding too aggrieved. Valerie showed the men out and they departed with cordial thanks and apologies for disturbing her at a difficult time. One of them said he hoped her mother would be better soon.

'Thank you,' said Valerie, 'she's recovering slowly. This was her second heart attack. It makes you realise how vulnerable we all are.'

'Indeed it does,' said the senior officer. They went away then and Lucy watched the colour come slowly back into her father's face. He looked at her with almost subservient gratitude.

'Lucy, you were wonderful!'

'Think nothing of it,' she said. 'You can do the same for me one day. I shall make sure you bloody well do.'

'Language, Lucy!' her mother said, coming back into the room.

'Leave her,' said Ian. 'She's a good girl.'

'Real!' said Lucy, 'This I like.'

'What was all that about?' Ben asked.

'That's what I'd like to know,' said Valerie.

'A case of mistaken identity, I suppose,' said Ian.

'Scary!' said Ben.

'Very scary,' said Ian.

'I've never seen you scared before,' said Lucy. 'I didn't know you were that human. I think I could really get to like you.'

47~

Piers arrived under cover of dark. This time David was not with him.

'Where's the body-guard?' asked Una

'In the car,' Piers strode into the house.

'Food, drink, coffee?'

'No,' he said, 'I may not have time for any of that.'

'What's the matter, Piers?'

Prune had heard his voice and hurled herself down the stairs and at him shouting,

'Piers! Piers! Piers!' He gave her a brief hug and they all sat down at the kitchen table, Una and Prune in their dressing-gowns.

'I have to find Eden,' said Piers. 'Do you know where he is?'

'No,' said Una, and then, 'I think you'd better go back to bed, Prune.'

'Oh, NO!' said Prune, outraged. 'I never see him. I want to stay up.'

'Prunella!' said Una, 'BED!' Prune slunk away slowly, sliding her slippers along the floor in protest.

'I'll come again, Prune,' said Piers.

'You always say that,' said Prune sulkily, 'but you don't do it.' She went out of sight up the stairs and Una said,

'I'm very worried. It's a long time since we've had word and I have a bad feeling about it.'

'I know he was onto the Elitists. He sent me an X-mail in code. Only part of it got to me. It ought to have been enough to incriminate the lot of them. I've been at MI5 all day arguing the point. But you know what they're like. One man's word in a partially deciphered coded message is not enough for an international operation of the kind they're normally engaged in.'

'So what will be the outcome of all this? Does it involve Hugo Finch?'

'Oh, yes. But if the ES have got to Eden first we may none of us ever know the outcome. They seem to be able to cover up anything.'

'What sort of thing are they covering up?'

'Don't ask.'

'What kind of cover up are they using?'

'Concealing the evidence. Eden informed me that all the evidence was contained in the papers hidden in a safe in the house of the man called Ian Derbyshire.'

'So. Can't they get a warrant to search his house?'

'It's been done. The safe was empty. We have no evidence at all at the moment. We know what they're doing but we have to have evidence. Ian Derbyshire's the ES treasurer. His records must contain all the evidence but he seems to be one step ahead of us.'

Prune began to walk slowly down the stairs. Half way she stopped in a commanding position. She gave a little, important cough. Piers and Una turned to look at her.

'Do you want the papers that were in Ian Derbyshire's safe?' she said.

'Go back to bed, Prunella,' said Una. 'Or I shall be very cross with you.'

'I'm talking to my brother, thank you very much,' said Prune.

'What did you say?' Piers was looking at her blankly. He was very tired after a day of unsuccessful negotiations with the senior officers at MI5. He realised she must have been listening. 'Do as Una tells you, Prune,' he said. 'Be a good girl. I'll come up and say good night before I go.'

'You mustn't go without the papers,' Prune said importantly.

'What papers?'

'The papers out of Ian Derbyshire's safe.'

'You don't know anything about this, Prune.'

'Yes I do. I took all the papers out of Ian's safe before I left the Derbyshires' house. I knew Eden wanted them and I wanted to punish Ian for being beastly to me. I brought them here in my back pack and I put them in the stone chest out there.'

No great actress had ever made a more meaningful gesture of triumph and defiance. Piers stood up.

'Is this one of your stories, Prune?'

'No. It's TRUE! Go and look.'

48~

When the officers from MI5 came to Ian's house for the second time they were not interested in searching. They had a warrant for his arrest. At the same time officers were arresting Hugo and Anthony Partridge. The charges ranged from racism to abduction and cannibalism. Valerie saw it as a mercy that her children were at their school house when the arrest was made. She was determined to remain calm for their sakes.

Isabel Finch was distraught. She began to question Hugo when she heard the charges, unable to believe them. Eventually, he yelled at her, asking her what she had thought she was eating at the centenary dinner. That silenced her. For the rest of the day and the following night she was unable to stop sobbing and intermittently vomiting.

Anthony Partridge accepted his arrest with dignity as befitted his position as President of the Society. He had no wife to be discredited with him. He knew what his fate and all their fates would be. They would not only face a prison sentence but would lose for ever their Insider status. It seemed to him that one or other punishment might be reasonably fair, but not both. He deeply grieved in custody over his loss of Pinecott Cedars. The house had been put in his name as most of the purchase price had been old family money of his own. He loved the place and could not bear the thought of being debarred from it or having it snatched from him and sold. No doubt the government would take possession of it now and it would be a rehabilitation centre or a hospital for feckless Outsiders. The very idea sickened him.

The Headmaster of Eton was more grieved about the loss of his position. His wife too was frantic with shock and grief at what had happened. She too was distraught at having been present at the ES centenary dinner.

The Chief Whip attempted to pull rank and asked for the protection of the House against the slanderous statements that were being made against him and his fellow Elitists. His word meant nothing now. His protestations only served to stir up the media to longer and more extensive coverage than they might otherwise have given to the events. It was a horrific and shameful end to a society whose Elitism had been a criminal hedonism without integrity, humanity or morals.

49~

The Agent had tried every reasonable measure to persuade Eden to give him the key to the code. He was determined to decipher the sheet that had been sent to the First Minister by his seemingly estranged half-brother. Eden had withstood all the persuasion and all the threats that had been offered him. Unlike most people he was unaffected by offers of money or the chance of a house in a compound and guaranteed Insider status. He was a little more perturbed when his sister was mentioned as a possible target but the Agent did not want to encumber the ES with more hostages. Keeping people incarcerated tended to lead to bad publicity and this was the last thing the Agent wanted for the Society. He also hoped to draw the line at blood and violence. After all he only needed the key to a code. There was no code in the world that was not decipherable given time. But he did not have time. If the society were to be saved from exposure, he had to know how serious Eden's information was. He hated unnecessary killings. He saw himself as a civilised man who sought to do good.

On the morning when, unbeknown to him, Hugo Finch and Ian Derbyshire had been arrested, he descended to the basement of Pinecott Cedars and let himself into Eden's cell. He had set the under floor temperature to something colder than would be easily bearable. He knew the level that was likely to cause death from hypothermia. He had set the level just above that. He had also taken the precaution, at gun-point, of removing Eden's clothing and had ensured that the bed was locked into the wall so that, if he wished to sleep, he would have to lie on the bare floor. Now he hoped the man would be a little more cooperative.

Eden was lying in the foetal position. His involuntary shivering looked promising.

'Are you ready to help me this morning?' The Agent went over to him and stood looking down at the fit, strong body. It was sad to see a healthy man in the prime of life reduced in this way. 'I'm sure you'd like a warm drink. Some nice hot coffee?'

'You bloody know I would,' muttered Eden.

'I'll fetch you a drink and then we can talk.' He went away and returned in a little while with a steaming mug of aromatic coffee. 'Get up,' he said, not unkindly. Eden struggled to his feet. 'Now,' he said reasonably, 'I'm sure you've had enough of this. I'm a reasonable man and so are you. All I want is the key to the code. Give me that and you can go home and forget all about this, hmm?'

'No,' said Eden and the Agent dashed the boiling liquid at his genitals.

He had left Eden and returned to the ground floor when he heard the warning siren that had been activated by the gate guards. Within seconds a small fleet of police vehicles was approaching along the front drive. He ran to a rear window. The same had happened there. The vehicles were parking and several armed men were getting out of a dark van. The Agent knew the property well. He knew that his only advantage was in the fact that, at present, the police did not. He made his way to the far end of one of the wings where an elegant pair of French windows opened in the shade of a number of cedar trees. The trees that gave the house its name. He unbolted the French windows and waited. He could hear shouting but no officer was yet in sight of this exit. The Agent opened one window, slipped out, closed the widow and went quickly to the nearest of the trees. They had huge trunks. He leaned against the tree on the side furthest from the house. He stood there for along time. Later in the day he moved to a larger tree that was further into the copse. It had broad, low branches and, taking off his shoes and socks, the Agent climbed up and was soon concealed from sight of anyone in or near the house by the dense foliage. He saw many of the staff of the Society taken away. He saw the chef and the kitchen-staff arrested and put into a van. He saw the factory farm manager taken away in handcuffs. Much later he saw a dishevelled Eden Diamond, wrapped in a coat and a blanket, taken away in a police car at speed. Finally, he saw the police vehicles drive away. When it was dark and the house stood empty without a single lighted window, the Agent descended from the tree and put on his socks and his shoes and walked down the drive and out through the unguarded gates.

50~

Ebbie had never got on with her mother. That was why they had lived apart for so long. Coming back had not changed things. Ebbie was as fanatical as ever about cleanliness and her mother lived on the edge with little concern for how she looked or whether her room was clean or tidy. After an escalation of rows and bitter recriminations Ebbie announced that she was going back to London.

'Where will you live?' Julia asked.

'With you, I hope,' said Ebbie. 'Don't you want to come?'

'In a way, yes, but London scares me.'

'I don't know if you'll think I'm mad,' said Ebbie, 'but I thought we might go back to Gareth's. We could offer to keep house for him and cook and things. He needs looking after.'

'And if he doesn't want us?'

'He'd give us a bed until we could find something else. He didn't go to all that trouble to save us only to throw us out on the street in the end.'

'Oh, I don't know, Ebbie. People don't want to be saddled forever with people they've helped. He gave us our freedom. He didn't ask us to cling on to him forever.'

'We won't know if we don't ask.'

'That's true. All right. I'm willing to give it a try. But he may not want both of us.'

'Maybe not, but you're the one who loves him so he ought to want you.'

'What did you say? How dare you say that?'

'I've got eyes in my head. I know how you felt. I know how you go on and on talking about him, even now.'

'He did a lot for us. We owe him everything.'

'I know that. I'm grateful too, but I didn't fall in love with him.'

'Shut up. Just shut it, okay?'

'If it wasn't true you wouldn't be so cross. I know that, see. So stop denying it.'

They went back to Wimbledon a few days later. The front door had not been mended and there were some Outsider squatters in residence. Julia was for going away again. There was no sign of Gareth and none of the squatters had ever heard of him. But Ebbie was not to be put off. She strode into the house and yelled at the squatters. She made completely unfounded claims to the property on her own and Julia's behalf and, within the hour, the house was empty. Together the girls mended the broken door panel. The lock still worked. The gunfire had only shattered the glass, allowing the Agent and his men to get in. The shots had been a scare-tactic. They could as easily have broken the glass with a stone or a fist. The house was as damp as ever and filthy from the squatters. Ebbie was in her element cleaning it up. The shed was empty, there was no sign that Gareth had been back since the day of their escape. They had no idea what had happened to him. Both feared he might be dead and neither voiced that fear to the other. They registered at the local allowance office and began a quiet and frugal life in the house together.

It was a long time before either of them suggested cleaning the secret room. Once it had been mentioned it loomed over them as an unavoidable duty and eventually they went there together and began the task of removing the remaining evidence of their days in hiding. In the midst of this work Julia sank down on the mattress where they had sat huddled together in fear and burst into tears.

'I'm afraid he's dead,' she sobbed. She did a lot of crying after that day and Ebbie comforted her as best she could.

One or two letters came for someone called Eden Diamond. The girls kept them in a pile near the door. They did not know what to do with them. Old-fashioned mail was a rarity and they felt slightly in awe of it. Only when they had lived in a compound had they ever received letters and then only very few. Finally, a letter came with the emblem of the World Government on its envelope. This too was addressed to Eden Diamond. They put it on the breakfast table and stared at it.

'I think we should open it,' said Ebbie. Julia was reluctant. 'We could steam it open and then stick it up again. We have to know what to do about this one, even if it only means sending it back.'

In the end, after a lot of argument, the girls opened the letter. It was from the First Minister himself. It asked 'Eden' to get in touch about a mail sheet in code. It said that part of the message was missing. It was signed, 'Your affectionate brother, Piers.'

'It's him,' said Julia. 'That code he was working on. I had to send it to Piers Diamond. That's his brother.'

'Whose brother?'

'Gareth's. Gareth is not just a secret agent. He's Eden Diamond.' Tears began pouring down her face. 'He's the brother of . . . of the First Minister of the World Parliament. He'll never want to marry me.'

'You're getting a bit ahead of yourself there,' Ebbie said.

'What are we going to do?' Julia wailed.

'We're going to stay here. We're going to look after his house and, if he's still alive, he'll find a nice home waiting for him when he comes back.'

'And what if he's not 'still alive'?'

'Then we have somewhere nice to live and no one can stop us.'

'Supposing those men come back - the Agent and his lot?'

'They won't. I'm afraid I think it was Eden Diamond they wanted, not us.'

'He saved our lives.' Julia was crying desperately.

'I know he did. He's a very brave man. He's also very clever.'

'Do you think we'll ever see him again?'

'Yes,' said Ebbie. 'I do. I really do.' And she was right.

51~

Prune had been trying all the morning to throw a ball over the house. It ought to have been easier at Una's. The main part of the house made throwing a ball and running through impossible because there was no doorway in line with the main front door. But the house was built round three sides of a square and one of the side wings, which had only one storey, could have been made for the game. Prune tried and tried but it was her throwing that was the problem. She simply could not seem to throw straight. It was a bit sad playing this game alone. She hoped one day to play it again with Ben and Lucy. She missed them a lot. She also missed Eden but Una had said that Eden was a law unto himself and must not be worried about or grieved for. Prune tried not to grieve but it had been a long time and she was afraid, from the quiet way Una spoke of him, that they would never see Eden again. She gave the ball a hefty chuck and set off, panting with effort and determination. As she emerged from the door on the far side she stopped in her tracks. Eden's bicycle was leaning against a tree.

A second later she heard him laugh and saw him walking towards her and then the ball came down and hit her on the head. It bounced off and Eden caught it deftly in one hand.

'Ouch,' said Prune and a second later they were hugging each other and dancing.

'Why didn't you phone?' said Prune, angry in her relief.

'I was going to phone for a lift from Reading station but I found my bike chained up in the yard so I came on that.'

'Where have you been all this time?'

'In hospital for a bit. Before that - you don't want to know. I was with some very nasty people.'

'Who?'

'I'm afraid your Mr Ian Derbyshire was one of them.'

'I could have told you that. I knew he was nasty.'

'Well, he's in prison now and I don't think they'll let him out in a hurry.'

'Are Ben and Lucy in prison too?'

'No, Prune, we don't imprison children because their fathers are bad.'

'So are they still there in their nice house?'

'I don't think so. I don't think they'll have a very nice house any more.'

'That's a pity,' said Prune. 'I liked them.' Eden took her hand and together they went indoors to find Una.

52~

A few years later, when Prune and the two cats from Wimbledon had been living contentedly at Una's, one of the cats became ill. Una thought there was very little hope but Prune was so determined that he must be cured that she agreed to go to a vet she knew of, who was doing very good work in an outsider district near Maidenhead. They went in Una's still battered vehicle, which continued to be serviceable, although it had been on its last legs for years, and the poor cat protested loudly all the way.

'When we come back you'll be all better,' Prune kept saying to him, with a touching faith that Una knew to be unfounded. As she had feared there was no help for the cat, who had lived more than his three score and ten in cat years, and was obviously in constant pain. The vet offered to keep him and 'do what was necessary'. Prune said a tearful goodbye to the cat and the vet called his assistant to see them out. The assistant had put her arm round the weeping Prune before they recognised each other. Then Prune looked up into the sympathetic face and shouted,

'Lucy!'

Lucy had been working as a veterinary assistant for nearly a year and was hoping eventually to do a full training to become a vet herself. She was delighted to see Prune and was able to give good news of Ben who was completing his education stoically and, even though they were now having to live in Outsider accommodation, had good and caring teachers.

'How is your mother?' Una asked, having introduced herself and been recognised as the godmother that Lucy had heard so much about in the past.

'She's as well as can be expected,' Lucy said. 'All that happened with Dad really knocked the stuffing out of her. I'm doing my best to look after her.'

'I'm sure you are,' said Una. 'If I can help in any way, please let me know.'

'Thank you,' said Lucy, and meant it.

'Can Lucy come home to tea with us?' said Prune, her grief forgotten.

'Of course she can, if she's free.'

The vet saw to it that Lucy was free and the three of them set off together. Prune insisted on sitting with Lucy in the back seat. On the way they passed a hydraulic lift working on one of the electric pylons.

'I wonder what's going on there,' Lucy said, not expecting an answer.

'I happen to know all about it,' said Una, 'I believe they're putting solar panels on the pylons in a way that will very soon cut the cost of electricity to a tenth of what it is now.'

'How do you know that?'

'I happen to know the scientist who invented the idea, and the man who made its implementation possible.'

'Don't tell me. I can guess who that man is. You people are so awesomely well connected!' said Lucy. 'I used to think it was impressive that my father knew the Chief Whip, but that was nothing compared to you. And now . . .'

'I can throw a ball over the house,' said Prune.

'And can you catch it on the other side?' Lucy asked quickly.

'Not yet,' said Prune, 'but I keep on trying. I never give up.'

'Real!' said Lucy, and hugged her.

'I'm glad we found you again,' said Prune.

'So am I,' said Lucy. 'Really, really glad.'

About the Author

Monica Shallis founded Cygnet Training Theatre and her life was dominated by theatre and music, lived in a constant stream of creativity. Both her musical and writing abilities were noticed at an early age and she took her LRAM and LGSM while training to be an actor. Words and music became her life and she had a successful career in the theatre before her love of teaching – of sharing knowledge – led her into schools in and around London and eventually to Exeter, where she remained for the rest of her life, and where Cygnet is based.

A keen and enquiring mind, coupled with a voracious 'seeking after truth' gave her an encyclopaedic knowledge in philosophy, poetry, religion and psychology (Jung being a figure of supreme importance for her, as were Shakespeare and Beethoven). In the late 70s Monica became an examiner for the Associated Board of the Royal Schools of Music, a position of which she was extremely proud and it was a great grief to her latterly that she became unable to cope with the travelling that was involved.

In many ways a 'Renaissance' figure, in addition to her writing, Monica designed and made masks and costumes, designed posters, painted stage sets, delighted in photography and used her vivid, boundless imagination in all aspects of her work. She adapted several great novels for the stage, including *The Woman in White* and a musical version of *Great Expectations*. She also wrote plays under a variety of noms de plume, many of which were written especially for, and performed by, the Cygnet company.

She leaves a huge body of work as yet un-published. *Piers Diamond* is her first novel.

Made in the USA
Columbia, SC
08 May 2017